DEAD IN THE MORNING

"Work it out for yourself," said Patrick. "They all had to jump to it when the old girl whistled."

"Yes, but to murder her? Lots of people have tiresome relations, but they don't kill them."

"People are seldom what they seem. Behind the facades of these prim villas and gentrified cottages in Winterswick many a drama must go on."

"No, Patrick. People are basically decent."

"Except when being decent interferes with what they want. Then they become ruthless."

D0733736

BANTAM BOOKS offers the finest in classic and modern English murder mysteries. Ask your bookseller for the books you have missed.

Agatha Christie

DEATH ON THE NILE
A HOLIDAY FOR MURDER
THE MYSTERIOUS AFFAIR
  AT STYLES
POIROT INVESTIGATES
POSTERN OF FATE
THE SECRET ADVERSARY
THE SEVEN DIALS MYSTERY
SLEEPING MURDER

Carter Dickson

DEATH IN FIVE BOXES
THE SKELETON IN THE
  CLOCK
THE WHITE PRIORY
  MURDERS

Catherine Aird

HENRIETTA WHO?
HIS BURIAL TOO
A LATE PHOENIX
A MOST CONTAGIOUS GAME
PASSING STRANGE
THE RELIGIOUS BODY
SLIGHT MOURNING
SOME DIE ELOQUENT
THE STATELY HOME
  MURDER

Patricia Wentworth

THE FINGERPRINT
THE IVORY DAGGER
THE LISTENING EYE
MISS SILVER COMES TO
  STAY
POISON IN THE PEN
SHE CAME BACK
THROUGH THE WALL

Elizabeth Lemarchand

BURIED IN THE PAST
DEATH ON DOOMSDAY

Margaret Erskine

THE FAMILY AT
  TAMMERTON
NO. 9 BELMONT SQUARE
THE WOMAN AT
  BELGUARDO

Margaret Yorke

CAST FOR DEATH
DEAD IN THE MORNING
GRAVE MATTERS

Ruth Rendell

A DEMON IN MY VIEW
THE FALLEN CURTAIN
A SLEEPING LIFE

June Thomson

ALIBI IN TIME
CASE CLOSED
THE LONG REVENGE

E. X. Ferrars

ALIVE AND DEAD
EXPERIMENT WITH DEATH
FROG IN THE THROAT
LAST WILL AND TESTAMENT
MURDERS ANONYMOUS

DEAD IN THE MORNING

Margaret Yorke

BANTAM BOOKS
TORONTO · NEW YORK · LONDON · SYDNEY

This story is a work of fiction and any resemblance
to real people is coincidental

*This low-priced Bantam Book
has been completely reset in a type face
designed for easy reading, and was printed
from new plates. It contains the complete
text of the original hard-cover edition.*
NOT ONE WORD HAS BEEN OMITTED.

DEAD IN THE MORNING

*A Bantam Book / published by arrangement with
the Author*

PRINTING HISTORY
First published by Geoffrey Bles Ltd. 1970
Arrow edition 1976
Bantam edition / October 1982

*All rights reserved.
Copyright © 1970 by Margaret Yorke.
Cover art copyright © 1982 by Bantam Books, Inc.
This book may not be reproduced in whole or in part, by
mimeograph or any other means, without permission.
For information address: Bantam Books, Inc.*

ISBN 0-553-22858-7

*Bantam Books are published by Bantam Books, Inc. Its trademark,
consisting of the words "Bantam Books" and the portrayal of a
rooster, is Registered in U.S. Patent and Trademark Office and in
other countries. Marca Registrada. Bantam Books, Inc., 666 Fifth
Avenue, New York, New York 10103.*

PRINTED IN THE UNITED STATES OF AMERICA

O   0 9 8 7 6 5 4 3 2 1

To my mother, Alison Larminie,
with love

FRIDAY

I

The only sound in the room came from an ornate clock on the mantelpiece as it marked the passing seconds with sharp, relentless clicks.

It was twenty minutes to three.

Mrs. Ludlow sat fidgeting in her chair. Everyone else was out, except Mrs. Mackenzie the housekeeper, who had wheeled her into the lift and transported her downstairs after her daily rest; now she was in her room, doubtless writing today's instalment of the fat bulletins she posted twice a week to her married daughter in Winnipeg. It was a marvel how she found so much to say.

There was nothing to do. Irritably, Mrs. Ludlow fumbled with the knobs of the portable radio that stood on the table beside her, among a heap of books, playing cards, photographs and letters. A droning voice filled the room, and some moments went by before Mrs. Ludlow understood what the monotonous tones were describing: the joys of making tomato chutney, seasonable now that it was too late for the fruit to ripen out of doors.

"Ugh, twaddle," said Mrs. Ludlow, who had never made a pot of any preserve in her life. She switched off the radio and drummed her fingers on the arm of her chair. Whom could she ring up? Who was at home now, to answer if she dialled them? She frowned, staring out of the window. It was a sunny day in late September, a day for the garden; presently Mrs. Mackenzie would wheel her out, with a rug tucked over her thin old knees, for a little air before tea, but meanwhile there was nearly an hour to occupy.

Where was Phyllis? Mrs. Ludlow couldn't remember. She

tried to recollect what day of the week it was. Her own routine never varied; only that of the other members of the household changed from day to day.

Yesterday Mrs. Mackenzie had gone to London, so it must have been Thursday, her day off. She always went to visit her son who had a tobacconist's shop in Clapham. Today was therefore Friday, and Phyllis must at this moment be in Fennersham having her hair done, for that was how she spent every Friday afternoon, and a great waste of time and money too, thought her mother; she always came back with her grey hair tinted a ridiculous ashen shade, and her face and neck flushed brick red by the drier.

Cathy was out playing tennis. It was just as well to have the child kept busy today, thought Mrs. Ludlow, at last admitting what was on her mind. She picked up a letter from the table and read it for the twentieth time. She could see perfectly without spectacles, but seldom subjected her eyes to strain, for one of Phyllis's duties was to read to her for hours at a time, often late at night after everybody else had gone to bed. Mrs. Ludlow enjoyed biographies of eminent Victorians, whilst Phyllis's own taste ran to historical novels which she lapped up one after the other in her bedroom, burning her light into the small hours. Her mother knew this, as she slept with her own curtains wide, and if she were wakeful could see the light from Phyllis's room shining across the garden, for the house was built in the shape of an L. She knew, too, that Phyllis's literary likes had not changed since she was a girl, a large, lumpy creature who spent hours lying in the garden immersed in a lot of romantic nonsense. Mrs. Ludlow had found her an unsatisfactory child, and was scarcely surprised that she had made a disastrous job of her adult life.

Her thin hand, the back mottled with large brown pigmentations, shook a little as she laid the letter back on the table. She was upset, and somebody else must be made to share her disturbance. She thought of Betty, her daughter-in-law, who lived five miles away on the other side of Fennersham, and who was sure to be out in the garden now, ferreting about among the weeds in the shrubbery or somewhere. It would be very annoying for Betty to hear the telephone bell and have to come indoors to answer it, doubtless scattering mud from her shoes as she hurried to the summons. She would naturally hear it, for an outside bell had been fitted for this very reason, so that Mrs. Ludlow might never call unanswered.

There was plenty to discuss. She could ask Betty about her sons. Tim was sure to be worrying her in one way or another, either by failing more exams, or by going about with long shaggy hair, garbed in fancy dress. Oxford seemed to be doing him no good at all. And Martin, Betty's elder son, had last year married an alarming girl with very short skirts and boot-blacked eyes who was bound to be leading him a dance by now. Altogether, Betty could be given a bad half-hour on the telephone before Gerald's letter need be mentioned. By the time all available topics for conversation had been exhausted, Mrs. Mackenzie would be ready to take her out in her chair, and if Betty were too down-hearted by then to go back to her garden, that was of no account.

Mrs. Ludlow stretched out her hand for the telephone.

II

Helen Ludlow gazed from the window of the Alitalia plane through gaps in the clouds at her first sight of England.

"It's like a patchwork, so neat," she said. "Aren't those meadows just tiny?"

The plane's engines changed their note as the run-in towards Heathrow began.

"You might see Windsor Castle, if you keep looking," said her husband. "It's a splendid curtain-raiser to this island."

Helen peered out at the doll-sized fields and houses spread below. Roads and rivers threaded them like ribbons, and match-box cars and lorries moved like marching ants.

"We'll soon be coming down," she said. "What time will we get to Pantons, Gerry?"

"About half-past nine, if the customs don't hold us up," said Gerald. "Nervous?"

"A little, I guess," Helen admitted. "What'll they think? After this long, your family will have had a real surprise. And Cathy may resent you getting married again. Supposing she doesn't like me?"

"She will, darling," Gerald said. He took her hand and clasped it firmly. "And everyone's had time to get used to the idea by now. We've been married three whole weeks, do you realise that?"

"I know it. Wonderful weeks," Helen sighed. Incredible, too.

"It will go on being wonderful," Gerald said. "This is just the beginning."

He sat relaxed as the plane slowly descended. This moment in a flight always made him think, not altogether incongruously, of the line from Deuteronomy, "Underneath are the everlasting arms," so aware did he become of the power of the machine in which he was travelling. He leaned back in his seat, holding Helen's hand, quietly content.

He had never expected, at his age, to have another opportunity of finding personal happiness. In the ten years since Cathy's mother died, he had managed well enough, dividing his time between the flat in London and Pantons, where he had a weekend cottage converted from the former stables. Cathy lived in the big house, cared for by her aunt Phyllis and criticised by her grandmother, while Gerald carried on two distinct lives. In the country his existence was calm and uneventful, in London much more hectic, marked with transient diversions; there had always been women, but he had never been able to feel more for any one of them than a physical attraction occasionally reinforced by some casual affection.

Then he had met Helen, and the miracle had happened.

"I still marvel about coming into that shop just when you were in trouble over Cathy's present," Helen said. "What if I'd been a little sooner? Or a half-hour later?"

"I expect it was in our stars," Gerald said with a smile. "Mrs. Van Doren would say that."

"Yes, indeed."

Helen still felt that she was living in a dream. So much had happened, so fast, that it was hard to catch up with the reality of events. She had met Gerald in the spring. He had gone to Milan on business, and had taken a few days off to visit Venice, where he had never been. Helen was there with the rich American widow who was employing her as secretary, lady's maid and companion during her travels around Europe.

Gerald quickly fell captive to the magic of Venice, walking for hours along the narrow streets, pottering in and out of the churches, gazing from the bridges at the murky water below, and simply watching what was going on around him. Like every tourist, he wanted to take presents home, and he went into a jeweller's shop off the Piazza San Marco in search of something for Cathy. The high-powered salesmanship of the shopkeeper was obscuring his judgement when Helen came into the shop.

Gerald asked the *padrone* to attend to her, since he needed time to make his choice, and freed from the flood of effusive persuasion, he turned with relief to inspect in peace the trinkets set out on the counter.

Helen thanked him, and then launched into a torrent of rapid Italian. The shopkeeper treated her with deference, and produced a large parcel which she had come to collect. Flowery remarks passed back and forth during this exchange. Gerald was only vaguely aware of all this going on as he held a gold mesh bracelet in one hand and a necklace in the other, debating their relative merits.

"Thank you so much," Helen said to him, preparing to leave the shop with her parcel. "That was kind of you."

"Oh, not at all. I shall be here for ages," Gerald said despairingly. "I can't make up my mind what to buy."

For the first time, he really looked at her, and on impulse said, "Perhaps you would help me?"

"Well, surely, if I can," Helen said. "What's the problem?"

"I'm trying to find something for my daughter. She's nearly eighteen. I thought perhaps a bracelet, like this one? Or a necklace? I can't decide which she'd prefer."

Helen promptly set down her parcel and picked up the bracelet.

"It's pretty," she said. "What does your daughter look like?"

"She's small and dark," Gerald said, and added, looking at her, "a little like you."

"Well, then." Helen held out her wrist, and the shopkeeper, delighted, fastened the bracelet round it. "This is beautiful," she said. "Any young girl would think it just lovely."

It certainly looked perfect where it was.

"The necklace is more sophisticated," Helen said. "Your daughter might not be able to wear it so often, but she could use the bracelet all the time."

"You're right," Gerald said, greatly relieved. "I'll take the bracelet. You think that one's the nicest?"

They tried on several others, but in the end chose the first one. Gerald paid, and picked up Helen's parcel. They left the shop together.

"You speak very good Italian," he remarked. "Where did you learn it?"

"In college," Helen said. "I majored in modern languages. I thought I'd forgotten it after so long, but it's coming back. I certainly do enjoy being able to speak the language of the people."

"I envy you," Gerald said. "I've got just a smattering, enough to get by at a pinch, but I don't get much chance to improve. I come to Italy quite often for my firm, but my Italian colleagues are better at English than I am at Italian, so you can guess what we speak."

"You should practise," Helen told him with a smile. "It's a pretty language."

"Yes," Gerald said. "But they talk so fast I find it very hard to understand. Do you travel a lot? Europe seems to be very close to America now."

"It's closer to Boston than the Rockies are," Helen said. "I haven't been over before, but my employer knows Italy well. We've been touring Europe for the past six months."

"How very pleasant," Gerald said. "I thought the usual American way was to cram all the N.A.T.O. countries into three weeks."

"I guess that is the normal pattern, but Mrs. Van Doren is very rich, and she can take her time," Helen said. "She likes to get the atmosphere. And of course she buys souvenirs everywhere; that's what's in this parcel."

"Do you enjoy working for her?"

"Very much," Helen said. "She's a thoughtful person, and I've loved visiting all these different countries. We spent Christmas in Paris, just imagine." In a sudden burst of confidence she added, "Mrs. Van Doren's a great believer in what the stars foretell, and some days we have to get through a heavy programme because her horoscope's encouraging, and other days we don't stir out in case of disaster."

"What's today's forecast?" Gerald asked. "A good day?"

"Steady progress may be made today," Helen said demurely.

"Oh, good," Gerald said. "Let's help it on by having a drink, shall we? Have you time?"

Helen looked up at the great clock on the Torre dell'-Orologio above their heads.

"I guess so," she said, laughing. "Mrs. Van Doren rests till her martini at six."

So they sat at a table in the huge square watching the

fluttering pigeons and the strolling crowds, sipping Cinzano and listening to the rival orchestras vying with each other as they played nostalgic tunes on either side of them.

Gerald stayed in Venice for three more days, and in that time he met Helen on several other occasions, by appointment and by chance. She and Mrs. Van Doren were in the Basilica staring in appropriate wonderment at the Pala d'Oro while he did the same; he saw them admiring Mantegna's St. George in the Gallerie dell'-Accademia that afternoon; and the next day, in the cool interior of Santa Maria della Salute, he heard Mrs. Van Doren say, "Why, I declare, there's that good-looking Englishman again. I wonder who he is?"

Helen's reply was inaudible. She gave no sign of recognising him on these encounters, and though he took his cue from her, Gerald was disappointed. He thought their sight-seeing would have been enriched by being conducted à trois, but perhaps Mrs. Van Doren's stars did not favour converse with a stranger Briton that week. Helen agreed readily enough to meet him when she was free; on his last night Mrs. Van Doren had a dinner engagement at the Gritti Palace; he and Helen ate fritto misto in a little trattoria, and then took a gondola trip around the city. As their long, black vessel with its curving prow moved smoothly down the canals, rounding the corners with a melodic cry from the gondolier, neither thought the experience corny.

Before they parted, Gerald asked her if Mrs. Van Doren's trip would bring them to England.

"I don't know," Helen said. "Maybe in the fall. She hasn't fixed on what we're doing after Greece. We go to Athens next month."

"Will you write, Helen?" Gerald asked her gravely. He recognised, with something like dismay, that it had become necessary for him to keep in touch with her. "I want to see you again," he said.

"It's better not," Helen said. "It's been fun. Let's just leave it that way, Gerald."

She would not budge. Implacably she refused to answer if he wrote to her, or to give him any address where he might find her, nor would she promise to get in touch with him if she did come to England. Despondently, Gerald left her, but he could not get her out of his mind. When, in the summer, he had to go to Genoa and Turin, he took some leave after his business was done and stayed on in Italy. Cathy was in

France on a language exchange, so that this year he had no obligation to take her away for a holiday, and half mocking at himself, he set about trying to track down Mrs. Van Doren and Helen. For all he knew, they might be still in Greece.

He tried the American Express, and he telephoned the best-known hotels in Rome and in Naples, with no success, but in Florence he found the trail. They had passed through, bound for Assisi, and in that small town he caught up with them at last. He had no difficulty at all in locating their hotel and securing a room there for himself.

This time, Mrs. Van Doren's stars had prophesied a pleasant encounter. Recognising Gerald, she bowed graciously towards him in the hotel dining-room while Helen, crimson-cheeked, bent intently over her soup. Later, Mrs. Van Doren invited him to have coffee with them; afterwards they strolled together down the hill towards the monastery, Gerald gallantly supporting Mrs. Van Doren on one arm, but aware only of Helen's nearness on his other side. He accompanied them, the next day, along the cobbled streets to see the tiny cell where Il Povero was imprisoned by his father to encourage him to recover from his religious obsession; they visited the tomb of St. Clare and saw her mummified remains, gruesomely visible behind a grille; they stood below the Rocca Maggiore in the gentle wind and surveyed the soft Umbrian landscape spread out below. Gerald got an extension of his leave. Another chance had come his way and he was determined not to let it go. He told Helen that he would not leave Italy without her.

Surprisingly, Mrs. Van Doren was his ally. She made various calculations to do with the position of the planets at their births, and recommended them not to flout the stellar plan. In privacy, she told Helen that she would be crazy to pass up such an opportunity.

"You're pretty enough, my dear, but you're not a girl any longer, let's be realistic about that. A woman must have money, or a man. You like him, don't you?"

"Oh yes," Helen sighed. "I like him. That's part of the trouble."

In the end she was overborne. Mrs. Van Doren cabled a niece in California to come and take over Helen's duties for the rest of the tour, and here they were, on their way to meet Gerald's family.

"We've landed, darling," Gerald said. "You were miles away."

"Yes. Yes, I was," Helen said. She gathered up her handbag and her gloves. Apprehension filled her, and he saw it.

"Don't worry, darling. Everything will be all right," Gerald said. "You'll see."

III

Dr. Patrick Grant, M.A., D.Phil., Fellow and Dean of St. Mark's College, Oxford, and lecturer in English, crossed Fennersham High Street at grave risk to his life among the cars whose drivers were all looking to right or to left in search of parking space. On Fridays the small market town was crammed with shoppers stocking up for the weekend; no wonder his sister Jane had so eagerly accepted his offer to carry out her commissions.

He went into the chemist's shop to buy some humiliating requirements for his infant nephew, and stood patiently waiting to be served among a cluster of mothers with restive children, a very old man with a stubble of whiskers, and two middle-aged women.

"Mrs. Ludlow's tablets, please," said one of these older women briskly when her turn came. The name caught Patrick's attention. He searched about in his well-stocked mind for the connection. It was in some way associated with trouble, and soon he remembered young Timothy Ludlow, a Mark's second year man, slightly spotty, a muddled thinker, and up before the Proctors and then himself more than once last term. Now that he thought about it, the boy did come from Hampshire. Could this woman be his mother? He looked at her more sharply while she made some other purchases. She was a tall, striking woman wearing a bright green jersey suit; her ash-coloured hair was swept up round her head in a becoming manner; she wore glasses and had plain pearl studs in her ears.

Patrick had just finished this inspection of the lady when an assistant came forward to attend to him, and he read out the items on his sister's list. By the time he left the chemist's, finished the rest of the shopping, and returned to his car, it had been hemmed in on all sides by other cars and he could

not move it. Never one to waste energy on vain causes when
it was so often needed for essentials, he lit a cigarette and
settled down to wait for the return of the offending Land-
Rover driver who had double-parked beside him, meanwhile
opening a small book of modern verse he had in his pocket
and which he had been asked to review.

From time to time Dr. Grant looked up from his reading to
see how the traffic situation might be changing, and thus it
was that he saw the woman he had noticed in the chemist's
shop walking along the pavement towards him. Her step was
firm and decisive, like her voice; she was clearly someone
who knew what she was doing and went about it purposeful-
ly; no ditherer, she. Patrick watched her enter the Cobweb
Café, immediately opposite where he was parked. It looked a
pleasant little place, a replica of hundreds all over England,
selling home-made cakes and serving genteel teas. Patrick,
mildly curious about her Ludlow connections, waited for the
woman to emerge, but she did not reappear.

He glanced up and down the road. There seemed to be no
immediate relief for his traffic problems, and no sign of a
policeman or a traffic warden. He took his volume of verse
into the Cobweb Café, sat at a table by the window where he
could see what went on outside, and ordered a cup of coffee.

IV

Cathy Ludlow pedalled along the road from Fennersham
towards Winterswick. In one hand she held her tennis racket,
and a duffle bag containing the rest of her sports gear was
slung across her shoulder. She felt pleasantly stretched by
the afternoon's exercise, and very full of the large tea she had
eaten after the game.

Long shadows were slanting through the trees as she bicy-
cled slowly down the hill into the village. Winterswick was a
straggly cluster of dwellings, some of them dating back to
Tudor days with mellow tiled or thatched roofs and sturdy
beams supporting the walls. She passed the Vicarage, a red
brick Victorian edifice which had splendid large rooms and
many draughts within, and the Post Office, whose affairs
were conducted in the parlour of a bright yellow bungalow,
and rode on past the Rose and Crown and the village grocery.

Then she turned into the lane that led eventually to her grandmother's house, Pantons. There was a small council estate on one side of the road, and on the other a speculative builder had put up two rows of timber-faced houses which had been sold at high prices to commuters from London. Further on down the lane there were more cottages, some of them still occupied by farm workers, some owned by retired couples, and more by people working in London who preferred antique charm to contemporary convenience.

A smart white Rover 2000 was parked outside Reynard's, a white-painted wattle-and-daub cottage with a garden full of Michaelmas daisies, golden rod and dahlias. Cathy looked at the car with interest as she rode by. Jane Conway must have a visitor; that was nice, for her husband had been sent to America for three months and she was left with a young baby as her sole companion meanwhile. Cathy slowed up, peering inquisitively over the fence; she liked Jane, whom she had met in the library and the village shop, although she felt a little shy of her, since though Jane looked extremely young she nevertheless had a husband and a baby and must be Cathy's senior by several years at least.

Jane was in the patch of garden where she grew vegetables, cutting a lettuce. She stood up as Cathy passed, saw her, and waved. Cathy waved back, and pedalled on her way.

Pantons, the last house in the village and the largest, lay some three hundred yards further along the road. Cathy turned in between the white gates and went past the lodge where the gardener lived; through the window she could see the flickering light of the Bludgen's television. The trees that bordered the long drive were changing colour now; autumn was in the air, and Cathy felt a poignant sadness. After today, nothing would ever be the same.

Near the house the drive forked, and the left branch led into the cobbled yard in front of the Stable House. In this courtyard Bludgen kept tubs of geraniums blooming through the summer, and Cathy could smell them as she put her bicycle away before walking up to the big house. She had been planning to move into the Stable House since she had left school at the end of last term; she was quite old enough now to be there alone while her father was in London, and perhaps he would give up the flat if she were available to keep him company. But this resolution was no longer of any importance and she might as well remain where she was in her familiar room at Pantons, down the passage from Aunt Phyllis. Luckily the news of her father's marriage had arrived before she had mentioned her idea about moving to anyone.

Uncle Derek's car was already parked outside the front door. Cathy's heart began to thump a little faster. She entered the house by way of the kitchen, where Mrs. Mackenzie was busy preparing dinner.

"Ah, there you are, Cathy. I was hoping you wouldn't be late. It's caramel soufflé for pudding," said Mrs. Mackenzie. She was a plump, grey-haired woman with bright blue eyes and pink cheeks.

"Mm, scrummy," said Cathy. "Can I lick the bowl?"

"No, dear, there isn't time. You must go and get changed," said Mrs. Mackenzie. "You'll want to look your best."

"Yes," Cathy agreed. Her thin face flushed, and her dark hair fell forward in two curtains obscuring her large brown eyes as she leaned over to inspect the mixture in Mrs. Mackenzie's bowl.

"Cheer up. You'll be able to go to college now," said Mrs. Mackenzie, who had always agreed with Aunt Phyllis that she should if she could get enough 'A' levels, and this she had just done. It was Grandmother who did not approve of university education for girls, and who said that Cathy's duty now was to look after her father.

"I know. I keep thinking of that," Cathy said, brightening. "Isn't it awful of me?" She had been ashamed of the prompt way in which this consoling reflection had sprung into her mind the moment she heard her father's news.

"Not a bit of it. It's only natural," said Mrs. Mackenzie. "Now run along, or they'll be thinking you've got lost."

"All right. I'll come and see if you want any help when I'm ready," Cathy said.

When she had gone, Mrs. Mackenzie tipped the frothing soufflé mixture into its dish and put it in the oven, humming under her breath. Then she took up the spoon again and with the tip of her pink, pointed tongue she licked off the sweet-tasting remnants that adhered to its surface; finally she spooned out and consumed every last tiny vestige of pudding that remained in the bowl.

V

"Who was that?" asked Patrick Grant, coming out of the door of Reynard's to speak to his sister. Jane, in faded jeans and a tartan shirt, stood in the vegetable patch waving at a young girl on a cycle who had just passed the cottage.

"It's Cathy Ludlow. A nice child, refreshingly old-fashioned," said Jane, stooping to pick some chives. "The big house at the end of the lane belongs to her grandmother." She indicated the direction in which Cathy was riding.

"Then it must have been her mother whom I saw in the chemist's shop," said Patrick. "A tall good-looking woman with ash-coloured hair. Rather elegant."

"That was Phyllis Medhurst," Jane told him. "Old mother Ludlow's daughter. Cathy's mother's dead. They both live at Pantons with the old girl, who's a regular tartar, from all accounts. I've never spoken to her, but I've often seen her out in the car. She's paralysed or something, spends her days in a wheel chair and leads them all the devil of a dance, according to gossip."

"Is there a Mr. Medhurst?" asked Patrick.

"Not any more. He departed some years back, I believe," said Jane. "I gather that Phyllis was always the dutiful daughter at home, unpaid secretary-cum-bottle-washer and general Cinderella, until the war. Then she managed to escape by joining the army or something. She went abroad and got married, but the marriage went wrong after the war so she came home, and has been there ever since, much gibed at by her mother, so I understand."

"Hm. We've a youth at Mark's named Ludlow," Patrick said. "Cathy's brother, perhaps? It's not a very common name."

"Her cousin. Cathy's an only child, but her uncle Derek has two sons and one of them's up at Oxford. Your lad, no doubt. I didn't realise he was at Mark's. Coincidence," she said. "One of your flock, is he?"

"Only in the general sense, like all of them," said Patrick. "He's reading P.P.E., as you might expect from his somewhat contemporary appearance."

"What a charming way of putting it," said Jane. "Can you really tell what subject they're doing by their looks?"

"It's not infallible. There are exceptions either way, but their styles reflect their interests," said Patrick. "You get the English scholar who goes in for Byronic curls and lace cravats, and historians who copy the hair-do of the Stuarts. I amuse myself harmlessly enough by noticing such details."

"You are an idiot," said Jane. "But I must say I hadn't thought of such a thing myself."

"Of course not. All you can think of these days is the needs of that tyrannic infant," Patrick grinned. "Tell me more about the Ludlows. That's a big house, isn't it? Do many of them live under the matriarchal wing?"

"Technically only Phyllis and Cathy. Cathy's father has a weekend cottage in what was the stables. The Derek Ludlows—your ones—live on the other side of Fennersham, but they have to drop everything and beetle over whenever the old lady blows her whistle, which is constantly."

"Perhaps she holds the purse strings," Patrick said. "Does Derek run the family business?"

"There isn't one, or not that you can notice," Jane answered. "Mrs. Ludlow's pretty rich, but I don't know where her money comes from. Derek's on the stock exchange, I think. I'm not sure what Cathy's father does, but he's some sort of tycoon. He goes abroad a lot."

"What happened to grandfather Ludlow?"

"He was killed in the First World War," said Jane.

"And your old lady's lived here ever since?"

"Yes. Ruling her family with a rod of iron," said Jane.

Patrick looked admiringly at his sister.

"How long have you lived in Winterswick, Jane?" he asked.

"Six months. Why?"

"I expect you know all about everybody else who lives in the village, too, don't you?"

Jane made a face at him.

"I do not," she said. "But the Ludlows live in one of the few big houses, and say what you like about the levelling down of society, their affairs are news. The old girl's quite a figure, you know, driving out in her car for the air, like a dowager duchess."

"I believe you're almost as inquisitive as I am," Patrick said.

"Oh no, I'm not. You're always looking for mysteries. I'm

just curious," Jane said. "I shouldn't waste your time brooding about the Ludlows, if I were you. There's nothing particularly mysterious about them. Pathetic, perhaps. Phyllis must have had a pretty depressing life, and it can't have been much fun for Cathy living all these years with her grandmother and her aunt, but she went away to school. She's rather bright, as a matter of fact."

"Only children often are," said Patrick. "They get heaps of undivided attention. It brings them on."

"You make them sound like ripening fruit," said Jane.

"Well, and so they are. All young things have to mature in time," said Patrick.

"Some people don't seem to me to be very mature when they're middle-aged," said Jane. "And there's some middle-aged excitement up at Pantons this weekend."

"I'm sure you mean me to ask you what it is," her brother said.

"Naturally," Jane replied. "It's Cathy's father. He's suddenly got married again."

"And do you feel that this is an impetuous, immature act?" asked Patrick.

"Not necessarily. It might be for the best. Why shouldn't he, after all? But it seems a bit impulsive. He met some female in Italy earlier this year and went chasing after her when his hols were due. He captured her, and they're coming here this evening."

"An Italian lady?"

"No, she's American. A widow, she was. If you stay glued to the window tonight you may see her go by. It's quite a thing for Cathy. I should think she's rather scared. It's not the same as if your father marries some childhood chum, or whatever."

"It's rather exciting, isn't it?" said Patrick. "I can see that Winterswick offers plenty of diversions for the mind, checking up on all the neighbours."

"Oh, you," said Jane. "You'd find diversions on a desert island, studying the sex-life of the crabs. I must leave you to your fascinating meditations now and go and feed your nephew. This greenery I'm clasping is for us, but supper won't be ready for an hour at least."

"In that case I think I'll just step down to the Rose and Crown for a while," said Patrick.

"You do that thing," said Jane. "And bring a bottle back with you."

VI

At Pantons, conversation during dinner on that Friday evening was sticky. Mrs. Ludlow, regal in the crimson lace dress that had been made for her grandson Martin's wedding, sat at the head of the table and ate a hearty meal; her digestion was excellent. Facing her sat her elder son Derek; he seemed absent-minded, not the genial uncle eager to listen to the tale of all her doings to whom Cathy was accustomed. She supposed that they must all be feeling the strain of the occasion. Aunt Betty had pinned her brooch on crooked and her lipstick was uneven. She wore a purple and white nylon jersey dress that clung to her too tightly, for she had put on weight. Cathy, who had always taken her kindly, untidy aunt for granted, suddenly saw her as she might appear to a stranger: frumpy, and rather ridiculous. What if Helen found her so?

Even Aunt Phyllis, who was often brisk but never unpredictable, seemed to be thinking of other things and did not answer when Mrs. Ludlow spoke to her.

"I said, are you sure they will have eaten, Phyllis?" Mrs. Ludlow repeated sternly.

"What? Oh yes, Mother. They'll have something on the plane. You always do," said Phyllis.

"And what do you know about that, may I ask?" inquired Mrs. Ludlow. "To my knowledge you have never taken to the air, Phyllis."

"Phyl's quite right, Mother," Derek said. "They will have eaten on the plane, and if for any reason the air line didn't feed them adequately, they'll stop for something on the way down."

"And keep us longer from our beds," grumbled Mrs. Ludlow, but the light of battle was shining in her eye. She had decided now how to play the hand, and Derek had been instructed to get two bottles of champagne up from the cellar and put them on ice, ready to greet the newly-married pair when they arrived.

"Well, I think it's all most exciting," said Betty with desperate gaiety. "Don't you, Cathy? I never thought your father would take the plunge after all this time, though I'm sure he must have had plenty of chances."

You don't know the half of it, thought Derek. He had often found much to envy in his brother's seemingly carefree bachelor life.

"Why isn't Tim here?" Mrs. Ludlow asked. "I thought you expected him home by now, Betty."

Betty's heart sank. She exchanged a glance with Phyllis. The sisters-in-law were good friends, both devoted to Tim, and they had often conspired to get him out of scrapes; too often for his own good, his mother was beginning to fear.

"He's back from Spain, Grandmother," she said. "Now he's staying with a friend." In fact, she had no idea where her younger son might at this moment be, but there was probably some truth in her reply. "What a delicious soufflé," Betty added, attempting to divert the conversation. "Mrs. Mackenzie really is a marvel."

"Is there any left? We ought to take it out to her before it collapses," Phyllis said. "You know how she loves puddings."

"That's why she's so good at making them, I expect," said Cathy. "Shall I take it?"

"Please, dear. Unless anyone would like some more?" Phyllis challenged with her eye anyone to dare, lest Mrs. Mackenzie should be deprived of her own portion.

"I will have just a little, Phyllis," Mrs. Ludlow said. "A spoonful, please."

There was hardly any left in the dish when Cathy took it to the kitchen. Mrs. Mackenzie was loading the plates and cutlery from the earlier courses into the dishwasher; on the kitchen table sat a yellow plate holding a large meringue, oozing cream: clearly she had not relied on any of the soufflé being left. Cathy was still giggling about this when they all left the dining-room after the cheese.

Mrs. Mackenzie had already put the coffee tray in the drawing-room. A nightly ritual was Phyllis's supervision of the Cona. Betty always admired this operation; she was impatient, and thought the quick results produced by a tin of instant coffee and a boiling kettle good enough. Nevertheless she appreciated the results of Phyllis's efforts. For once Mrs. Ludlow did not make critical comments on the strength or otherwise of the flame under the glass; when their cups were filled, no one had anything to say and they all sat round in silence, sipping.

"Well, my goodness me, what a lot of miserable faces," said Mrs. Ludlow, looking at them all. "Anyone would think

this was a funeral feast, not a homecoming. Why are you all
·so gloomy? Gerald's old enough by now, I hope, to know
what he's doing."

"It seems a little hasty, perhaps, Mother," Derek suggested. He glanced apologetically at Cathy. "Marry in haste and
all that."

"Ten years of widowhood is no short time, I do assure
you," said his mother.

"Derek means Gerald hasn't known Helen long, Grandmother," interpolated Betty.

"I know what Derek means," said Mrs. Ludlow testily.
"I'm sure we all wish Gerald to be happy."

"Of course we do, Mother," said Phyllis. She had been
very quiet all the evening. She and Gerald had always been
very close; the bond between them had been made stronger
by the fact that the marriages of both had ended, though for
different reasons, and Gerald had reason to be grateful to his
sister for her care of Cathy. She would be anxious about her
brother until she had got to know his wife; meanwhile a sense
of some intrusion was inevitable, but it was Cathy who would
be the more affected.

"It's an excellent thing to have happened, and I'm delighted,"
Phyllis said now. "The next thing is to think about getting
you into a university, Cathy. It's too late for this year, I
suppose. What do we do to apply for a place for next year?"

As she had intended, this hare stimulated everyone to
argument of one sort or another, so much so that they failed
to hear a car draw up outside, and voices were still raised in
discussion when the drawing-room door opened and Gerald
entered, leading Helen by the hand.

There was a silence. Cathy broke it, by springing up and
rushing to her father, crying, "Daddy, Daddy." She hugged
him, then fell back and looked at Helen in sudden self-
conscious embarrassment.

Helen held out her hand.

"Hullo, Cathy," she said gravely.

Cathy felt a rush of gratitude to her for not seeming to
expect a kiss. She shook hands, then stood aside to let Gerald
lead Helen up to Mrs. Ludlow. He bent to kiss his mother's
dry old cheek; she smelt of soap and *eau de cologne*.

"Here's Helen, Mother," he said.

"Well, let me look at you, child," said Mrs. Ludlow, staring at Helen intently. You could be so rude when you were

old and get away with it, thought Cathy. Gran was really awful, scrutinising Helen up and down minutely. "You're much too thin," was her pronouncement when she had completed this inspection. "I suppose you've been racketing about all over Europe. Now you must settle down and put on flesh."

"Mother, you mustn't be so personal," Gerald scolded. He was the only person apart from Dr. Wilkins who ever dared reprove Mrs. Ludlow. "Take no notice, darling," he added to Helen. "Mother loves to tell us all what we ought to do."

"And none of you pay the least attention," remarked his mother, but she smiled in a wintry way.

How did he do it?

Phyllis watched, fascinated, while Gerald went on talking to their mother. He could say anything to her and she would come back smiling; he teased her, and she enjoyed it. Yet the rest of them, who had to tend her and to deal with her each day, were all afraid of her, even Derek. It wasn't fair.

Her mother was not yet eighty. This might go on for years.

Phyllis pulled herself together as she heard her own name mentioned.

"Darling, this is my sister Phyllis. She's done so much for Cathy," Gerald was saying.

How did you greet a new sister-in-law, not a young woman, certainly, but a great deal younger than yourself? Phyllis was not demonstrative, but she was very fond of Gerald; she bent and kissed Helen primly on her pale cheek.

"I hope you'll both be very happy," she said in a stiff voice.

"Why, thank you, Phyllis," Helen said. "You know Gerry, so you'll know that I am very happy." And indeed she looked it now, smiling at them all with disarming shyness.

"Well said, well said," said Derek heartily. He advanced towards her. All this kissing seemed a bit much on first acquaintance, but he must follow his sister's lead; the sooner these greetings were over and they all settled down again to normal life, the better. He bent and pecked Helen's cheek in formal fashion, very relieved to see that his brother had not fallen for some dolly in a mini-skirt. Helen wore a white wool suit in which she looked elegant enough; she seemed, thus far, entirely suitable, though perhaps not very robust: Gerald must have a *penchant* for fragile women. It was to be hoped that Helen was physically tougher than her appearance indicated. With these reflections Derek turned thankfully to the task of opening the champagne.

"We've all been so curious about you, Helen," Betty said, coming forward in her turn. "Gerald hasn't told us anything at all. We'd no idea what to expect. Welcome, anyway."

"This is Betty, darling," Gerald said, somewhat superfluously.

"How do you do, my dear," said Betty, kissing her with warmth. "You mustn't mind me, I'm the tactless one."

Helen was saved from replying to this difficult introduction by the entry of Mrs. Mackenzie, who had come to take away the coffee tray.

"Ah, Mrs. Mack, how are you?" said Gerald breezily. "Helen, this is Mrs. Mackenzie, the best cook in the world. Mrs. Mack, my wife."

"How do you do, I'm sure, Mrs. Gerald," said Mrs. Mackenzie, smoothing her hands on her apron; she smiled pleasantly, looking at the newcomer, and then her expression changed. Cathy noticed suddenly what a piercing glance came from her bright blue eyes when she was interested. She could not be said to stare, in the sense that Gran did, but nevertheless she was summing Helen up just as shrewdly. Her gaze narrowed. The hand that she had been about to extend dropped to her side.

"I'll just take out the tray, madam," she said to old Mrs. Ludlow, picked it up, and left the room.

"What's bitten Mrs. Mack?" asked Gerald of the room at large. "Bit abrupt, wasn't she? And she's put on weight. Too many sweets, that's the trouble."

Derek was pouring out champagne.

"Come and get a glass, everyone," he said. "Gerald, give the girls their *vino*."

Of them all, only Phyllis noticed that Helen's already pale face had turned a chalky white.

SATURDAY

I

The Dean of St. Mark's sat in his sister's garden with a rickety deal table in front of him covered in papers. At his side was a foolscap pad on which he was writing busily. Occasionally he paused in his labours and gazed at the pram which stood some feet from him under the shade of an apple tree. An indolently waving arm or leg could usually be seen moving within it; his nephew Andrew, under his supervision, was spending a peaceful afternoon investigating his limbs.

Jane was out collecting for a flag day; one of Winterswick's older matrons had bullied her into undertaking this charitable act, and Jane had decided that if Andrew were left behind, she would get around her area more quickly. She had been gone for two hours, and Patrick pitied her, trudging round the village begging, while he sat tranquilly at work. All the same, if she did not return soon he would have to give Andrew his orange juice, for such were his instructions, and he was not too confident of his ability to carry out this mission without a clash of personalities.

He turned his attention once more to the mysterious disappearance from Chipping Campden in 1660 of William Harrison, and was absorbed in the details of this puzzling affair when he heard the garden gate open as his sister arrived home.

"Well, how have you been, my angel?" Jane crooned over the pram. "Has that bad uncle of yours forgotten all about you?"

Some cheerful gurgling sounds answered her.

"He's been extremely good," said Patrick. "Not a squeak, all afternoon."

"There, I told you he wouldn't be a bother," said Jane complacently.

"How have you fared? Fleeced the natives satisfactorily?" asked Patrick.

"Saturday afternoon's a bad time to get people at home," said Jane. "Lots of folks were out, but I did quite well, all the same. It was rather fun really, it's a chance to chat to people one might not otherwise meet. I met young Cathy Ludlow on her way to deliver a note at the vicarage, so I asked her back to tea. She'll be here in a minute. I thought we'd have it in the garden, if you'll clear a space."

"Very well," said Patrick meekly. He began to tidy up his papers, and Jane went into the house with her collecting box and tray of flags. As she came out again, Cathy appeared at the gate, pushing her bicycle.

"Ah, there you are, Cathy. Come along in," called Jane.

Cathy wheeled her machine through the gate and propped it against the hedge. Then she approached the others, looking rather shy.

"This is my brother Patrick. He's the Dean of St. Mark's, where your cousin is," said Jane. She bent over the pram and plucked Andrew from its depths. "Here, Cathy, you talk to Andrew and Patrick while I get tea," she said, and thrust the baby into Cathy's surprised arms.

"Oh, can't I help you?" asked Cathy, eyeing Andrew nervously.

"No, no. You sit down and amuse Andrew," Jane instructed.

Cathy sat down on the wooden garden seat, clutching the baby tightly. He was a writhing, squirming mass of concentrated energy, she discovered, but he beamed at her myopically, and dribbled.

"He likes you," Patrick observed.

"I'm afraid I'm not very used to babies," Cathy said. "I've never really met one socially before."

"Well, I'm glad I'm excused from giving him his tea," said Patrick. "If Jane hadn't come back by half-past four, that was what I had to do. I'm not used to babies either. But he's a good little chap, this one." Peering at the infant through his heavy-rimmed spectacles, Patrick gave him a friendly poke in the stomach. "I'd better clear up this mess before Jane comes back with the tea," he added, opening a big box file and piling his papers into it.

"Are you writing a book?" asked Cathy reverently.

"Not a whole book. Just a paper. I'm very interested in unsolved mysteries," said Patrick, "and there are quite a few that happened long ago and haven't been explained. I'm adding several thousand words of thoughts to what's already been said about the Campden Wonder."

"What was that?"

"He was a man who disappeared from Chipping Campden in 1660. Three people were executed for his murder, and then he turned up again, hale and hearty, two years later," Patrick said. "No satisfactory solution to the mystery has ever been given. Rather tough on the three scapegoats, too, don't you think?"

"Yes," said Cathy. "How extraordinary."

"Modern knowledge throws new light on a number of things that baffled our forbears," Patrick told her happily. "For instance, George III was a much maligned monarch. As you know, everyone thought he was mad, but now it's believed that he suffered from porphyria."

"Whatever's that?"

"A disease with symptoms similar to insanity. It was not recognised all those years ago. But present-day doctors, reading about poor old George's sufferings, find them typical of the illness."

"How very interesting," Cathy said.

"Yes, isn't it?" said Patrick. "Then there was Amy Robsart, who was found dead at the foot of the stairs of the house where she was living, with a broken neck. You remember who she was, the wife of the Earl of Leicester who was such a chum of Queen Elizabeth the First's. People thought she might have been pushed down the stairs, though the verdict of the day was misadventure. But it was strange that her body wasn't bruised, as you might expect after such a fall, and as they said at the time, the 'hood which stood upon her head' wasn't disarranged. A theory's been put forward now that she may have had a spontaneous fracture of the neck due to a secondary cancer. This is not uncommon, and it was rumoured that she was suffering from some severe ailment. Unfortunately her grave can't be found so that there's no hope of testing her skeleton to find out for sure. But the facts fit, and would explain what happened."

"Is this what your work is at Oxford?" asked Cathy.

"No, this is just a hobby," Patrick said. "My official subject's English."

Jane came back at this moment with the tea tray.

"Come on, Patrick," she exclaimed. "Haven't you cleared the table yet? I suppose you've been haranguing Cathy about Beowulf or something."

"Your brother's been telling me about the death of Amy Robsart," Cathy said. "It's fascinating."

"Patrick is the most inquisitive man ever to be born," Jane told her. "He looks for mysteries where there are none, and is always poking his nose into other people's business."

"To their advantage sometimes," said Patrick mildly. "I'll just take these papers into the house."

"He must be very clever," said Cathy when he had gone.

Jane looked surprised.

"Oh, not especially," she said, with the nonchalance of one whose relations were always expected to get brilliant firsts.

"I expect you're just used to him," said Cathy tolerantly. "He looks very learned."

"That's his specs," Jane said. "I used to think he took to them originally to furnish his face and make him seem older to the undergraduates, but he seems to need them now."

"I haven't heard Tim mention him," said Cathy. "I expect their paths don't cross, as he isn't reading English."

Jane forebore to mention that Patrick, as Dean, was responsible for student discipline and so had often come across her cousin.

"Where is Tim now?" she asked instead. She had set out the tea things, and put a rusk into Andrew's hand. The baby chirruped in a pleased way and began to gnaw it wetly.

"I don't know. He's been in Spain, but I think he's back from there. He's probably staying with some of his weirdie friends," said Cathy.

Patrick came back and sat down, and Jane poured out the tea.

"Hang on to Andrew while I do this, Cathy," she said. "Then I'll give him his orange juice. I was just asking Cathy where young Tim is," she added to her brother. "She doesn't seem to know."

"My uncle and aunt, Tim's parents, came to Pantons last night," Cathy said. "They don't know where he is at present, but he'll turn up."

"Of course he will," Patrick agreed. When his funds run out, he thought. "He's been away for most of the vacation, has he?"

"Oh yes," said Cathy. "I thought he had a lot of work to do, but he must have forgotten about that. I don't think he's written home very much. It's bad of him, because Aunt Betty anguishes about him and he ought to humour her."

"Young men are sometimes thoughtless," Patrick said.

Jane took her son from Cathy.

"Help yourselves, you two," she said, and began to spoon orange juice into the baby's mouth. "Cathy, tell us about your step-mother. How did you get on last night? Do you like her?"

"Jane, really! Now who's exhibiting vulgar curiosity?" expostulated Patrick. "Don't answer her, Cathy."

"Oh, I don't mind," said Cathy. "It's nice of you to wonder. She's rather nice. A bit shy, I think. She didn't talk very much, but it must have been pretty awe-inspiring for her, meeting everyone like that, and Gran too." She turned to Patrick. "My grandmother has arthritis and has to be in a wheel-chair, and she's rather a formidable person, a bit like the old lady in the Whiteoaks books, if you know who I mean. Alarming, even when you're used to her."

"Well, I'm glad you took to your step-mother," said Jane. "Perhaps I shouldn't have asked you to tea with us today, as she's only just arrived. You might have preferred to stay at home and get acquainted."

"Oh no," Cathy said. "I couldn't, anyway. Helen and Father have gone to London for the day."

"Oh?" Patrick's tone was interrogative, and Jane frowned at him.

"I was a bit disappointed when I heard about it," Cathy admitted. "But it seems Helen hasn't been to England before and she couldn't wait to see Buckingham Palace and the Houses of Parliament. They're coming back tonight and Aunt Phyllis and I are going to have drinks with them after dinner."

"Well, that will be pleasant," said Jane.

"Yes, it will," said Cathy. She had vigorously suppressed the hurt she felt because Father and Helen had not included her in their trip; she must get used to this exclusion, and not mind it. "It will do Gran good to have a quiet evening," she added. "She got a bit worked up last night and couldn't sleep. Aunt Phyl had to read to her for hours."

"She doesn't have a nurse?" asked Patrick.

"No, she isn't ill. Just immobilised. She has pills and things to calm her down or to keep her going. It must be pretty awful for her, if you think about it," Cathy said. "Mrs. Mackenzie—that's the housekeeper—is very good with her. She helps Aunt Phyllis get her dressed, and bath her, and so on. One of them's always at home."

"I met Mrs. Mackenzie in the Post Office this morning," said Jane. "I was mailing a letter to Michael by the first post, and she was sending a letter somewhere abroad too."

"I expect it was to her daughter in Canada," said Cathy. "She writes twice a week, as regular as clockwork, on Wednesdays and Sundays. But it's Saturday today, this must have been an extra one."

"Perhaps her daughter has a birthday coming up," Patrick said. "Is she Mrs. Mackenzie's only family? I wonder she doesn't join her."

"She's got a son, too. He lives in London. He's got a tobacconist's shop," said Cathy. "Mrs. Mack goes to see him every Thursday."

"A creature of routine, clearly," Patrick said.

"Yes," Cathy agreed. "She used to live in Canada; she often talks about the frozen Red River. It flows into the Arctic, so when it thaws it can't escape because the sea's still ice. They have bitter winters out in Winnipeg, she says."

"Lucky for you she prefers the English climate, then," said Jane.

"It is. I don't know what we'd do without her," Cathy said. "She's a super cook, and not many people would put up with Gran's ways. Not that she's really such a trial," she added hastily. "She's only old."

"Any independent person forced to rely on others can be forgiven for getting a little tetchy," Patrick said; rather pompously, his sister thought.

Later, when Cathy had gone, he asked Jane if she had taken her collecting-box up to Pantons.

"Not yet. I'm a bit scared of the old lady, as a matter of fact," admitted Jane. "I thought I'd go up after supper, when she might have gone to bed. The paragon Mrs. Mackenzie could no doubt cart my tin up to her bedside."

"I might do it for you, if you ask me nicely," Patrick said.

II

"I haven't finished yet," said Mrs. Ludlow crossly when Phyllis came into her room soon after eight o'clock that evening. The old lady was propped up in bed against a special upholstered back rest; she was dressed in a fleecy white bed jacket, and her short white hair looked like lamb's wool. Across her knees rested a tray-table, and she was shovelling chicken fricassee greedily into her mouth. "You know I hate my meals being disturbed," she added.

"I'm sorry, Mother. I just popped in to make sure you've got everything. Cathy and I are off now. You remember that we're going down to Gerald's, don't you?"

"Of course I remember. I'm not senile yet," snapped her mother. "Get along with you, then. And be pleasant to that young woman. She seems very timid."

"Helen? Yes, I'll do my best to be friendly," said Phyllis stiffly. Mrs. Ludlow was scarcely an appropriate advocate for amiability.

"She'll do Gerald a lot of good," the old lady added, with her mouth full. A grain of rice escaped and dropped on to the ridge of her bony chin. Phyllis felt a pang, watching her; poor old thing, she might be selfish and unkind, but she was so dependent and she was often in a lot of pain. Mrs. Mackenzie would clean her up, when she came to take her tray, if she had not adequately wiped her face by then.

"Is there anything you want, Mother?" Phyllis asked. "I put a pill out for you, in case you want to take one later."

"I know, I know. It's still there," said Mrs. Ludlow impatiently. "Did you think it had blown away?" One of her sleeping tablets, a bright blue capsule, lay on a saucer on the bedside table beside her, with a carafe of water and a glass. "Go along, Phyllis. Stop fidgeting."

Phyllis went, without another word.

"Silly girl," muttered her mother when the door had closed behind her. "No wonder that fool she married couldn't stand her."

Mumbling to herself, she went on eating. She finished all her chicken, scraping the fork round her plate till nothing remained. Then she lay back for a while, panting slightly.

She still felt a little over-excited, it was true; she might take that pill. On the other hand, if she were wakeful, Phyllis could come and read to her from the life of Gladstone that had just arrived from Harrods library. Now there was a proper man, if you like, even though the old Queen hadn't cared for him; different from some of the creatures calling themselves men today, her own son Derek for a start. Waffling and pompous, he was, and ineffectual. No wonder his boys had turned out badly. Martin looked almost girlish, with his fair hair and thin features; probably he had rushed into marriage with that ridiculous girl in an effort to prove himself, somehow. She tried to remember where they had met: ah yes, it was on a ski-ing holiday in Austria; foreign travel had much to answer for. A girl like that needed a strong tough man to tame her. And as for Tim, he was worse than his brother; he even had long hair. His parents seldom seemed to have knowledge of his whereabouts or doings; a fine state of affairs.

She thought about her husband. He had been dead for over fifty years; their sons and daughter were middle-aged. What would he think of them, if he could see them now? He would be disappointed in the elder pair for sure: an unsuccessful stockbroker, and a frustrated, childless woman.

"I tried, Gerry, I tried," Mrs. Ludlow said aloud. She often talked to herself when she was alone. "I did my best with them," she mumbled and her voice quavered.

But Gerald was different. He had spirit. He had prospered in his career, beginning in a lowly post in the firm where he was now a director; and his first marriage had been successful, too. It was ironic that death had ended it, and unfortunate that Cathy had been the only child. But now Gerald had found another wife. When Helen had called him Gerry in her hearing, the stony area that was Mrs. Ludlow's heart had been touched, for that was her name for his father. The girl loved him, and he loved her too; it showed in both their faces. So Mrs. Ludlow wished them well; Gerald could have more children, it was not too late; spunky ones with guts, like himself and Cathy, who was a girl to be proud of though it would never do to let her be aware of her grandmother's approval. The stock that bore the Ludlow name might yet improve.

Mrs. Ludlow looked at the tray on her knees. Lemon meringue pie, and a jug of thick cream: one of her favourite puddings.

III

The sitting-room in the Stable House was comfortably furnished with deep armchairs and a sofa covered in faded rose-coloured linen. There were a few good pieces of furniture: a walnut tallboy and a graceful regency table on which was arranged a great vase of Michaelmas daisies and yellow roses.

"This is how I'd always expected England to be," Helen said, gazing round the room. "I didn't really take it in properly last night. But now I've seen the sunlight on the old red bricks, and all the flowers growing in the garden, and that man Bludgen, bent double weeding, well, I guess I've arrived all right. You must have fixed those flowers, Phyllis; they're lovely. Thank you."

Phyllis said: "What do you think of London?"

"It's beautiful. All those ancient buildings! And the river! And the stores, too. Of course, we didn't have time to go in any place, we just drove around for a while, and we had lunch at the Savoy Hotel. That was quite something."

"I'll bet it was," said Cathy. She felt drawn to stare at Helen, but tried to hide her intense curiosity. Her stepmother wore a simple coffee-coloured dress; her hair was smoothly brushed into a long bob, and she looked superlatively elegant.

"Have you had dinner?" Phyllis asked. "Though after lunch at the Savoy you can't have been very hungry."

"We fixed some steaks out of the ice-box," said Helen. "It's the first time I've cooked anything for Gerry, Phyllis. I expect we have you to thank for getting in the groceries."

"Cathy and I did it together," Phyllis said. "We didn't want you to have to bother about shopping until you'd had a chance to settle down and find your way about. You'll be coming up to the house for lunch tomorrow. We have a custom that all the family gathers together for Sunday lunch. Mother expects it."

"Yes, Gerry told me," Helen said.

To Cathy it seemed strange to hear her father called by this diminutive of his name. It was endearing. Although Helen seemed so self-contained, she must be very fond of him. It all took a little getting used to.

A door led from the sitting-room directly into the kitchen, and at this moment it opened and Gerald came in, carrying a bowl of ice.

"Sorry to keep you all waiting," he said.

"We thought you'd gone to the well, Daddy," said Cathy. "You were ages."

"We're all panting for that drink, Gerry," Helen said, with the slow, sweet smile that transformed her face.

"It's coming up right away," said Gerald. "What'll it be for you, Phyl? Whisky?"

"Please."

Gerald set about preparing the drinks, and he had just handed Cathy her Dubonnet when the doorbell rang.

"I'll go," said the girl, springing up. She went out into the hall, and returned almost at once, beaming widely, and followed by a tall, well-built man with thick, straight dark hair and a pair of very keen hazel eyes behind heavy-rimmed spectacles. He carried a collecting box and a tray of flags.

"It's Dr. Grant," said Cathy. "I had tea at his sister's house today, I told you. He's doing some of her flag-day collecting."

"Why, come in Dr. Grant," said Gerald warmly. "I'm delighted to meet you. You know my nephew, I believe."

"I do," said Patrick, and added, "I apologise for intruding on this family occasion, but my excuse is that I want to help my sister, who has already spent hours tramping round the village for the good cause. I hope I can persuade you all to add a contribution?"

"Certainly," said Gerald. He took out his wallet and extracted a pound, which he rolled up and poked into Patrick's tin. Patrick gazed expectantly round, and Gerald introduced him to Helen and Phyllis.

"I'll just get my purse," Helen said, and left the room. Phyllis rummaged in her bag and found a florin.

"I put mine in this afternoon," said Cathy sunnily. "I bet Jane's collected more than they got last year. People would cough up better for her than for boot-faced old Mrs. Hunt who always used to do it."

Patrick shook the tin.

"It feels quite heavy," he said. "It can't be too bad, unless it's mostly pennies."

"You'll have a drink, won't you, Dr. Grant, now that you're here?" said Gerald.

Patrick accepted readily. He sat down beside Phyllis and spoke to her.

"I've seen you before, Mrs. Medhurst," he told her. "In Fennersham yesterday. I was shopping for my sister. You were in the chemist's."

Phyllis's face turned an ugly dull red.

"I didn't notice you," she said.

"Why should you? I heard the name Ludlow, and remembered the young man we have at Mark's," said Patrick.

"Tim. He arrived home unexpectedly this evening," Phyllis said.

"You'll meet him at lunch tomorrow, Helen," Cathy said. "A treat in store. Modern youth." She turned to Patrick. "All the family has lunch at Pantons on Sundays, Dr. Grant," she added. "Except Tim's brother, Martin, who's broken with tradition because his wife doesn't believe in such Victorian conduct."

"Really, Cathy," remonstrated Phyllis. "I'm sure Dr. Grant isn't the least bit interested in our family customs."

"But I am. I find these habits that survive through the generations very fascinating," said Patrick. He stood up as Helen came back into the room.

"I'm sorry I've been so long. I'm not used to your English money yet," she said. She was rather flushed. "I have some *lire*, and a few dollar bills, but not many English notes. Will this be all right?" She produced a ten-shilling note and gave it to Patrick, who put it in his tin.

"Splendid. Thank you," he said.

"Darling, you didn't have to go hunting about upstairs for that," Gerald said. "You've got me around now to see to such things."

"I'd have thought your pound was plenty for the whole family, Daddy," Cathy said.

Helen laughed. She looked rather embarrassed.

"I guess you're right, Cathy," she said. "Still, it's for a deserving charity, isn't it?"

"Cathy, since Dr. Grant is here, why don't we pick his brains about getting you into the university?" said Gerald.

"Oh Daddy! I didn't think we'd get round to talking about it for weeks," said Cathy. Her eyes shone and she looked expectantly from her father to Patrick.

"Well, you've really your aunt to thank," said Gerald. "She

wasted no time reminding me about your excellent exam results. What should we do, Dr. Grant?"

Patrick told him, at some length, and added an invitation to any Ludlows who cared to accept for luncheon in his rooms next term. Helen was delighted by this; she said that she had longed for years to visit Oxford.

"Helen's a most gratifying Anglophile; aren't you darling?" said Gerald. "I think she only agreed to marry me because it was a quick way to get to England."

"Well, I think it's wonderful that you should feel like that, Helen," said Phyllis firmly. "Nowadays, when so many people are saying that Britain is finished, it's very heartening to find foreigners, if you'll forgive me for calling you one, Helen, eager to settle here." She spoke with some passion, her colour high.

"Well done, Mrs. Medhurst," exclaimed Patrick admiringly.

"Well, it's what I feel," said Phyllis. "When you think of what happened during the war, it sickens me to think of how much national pride we've lost. It's like saying that all young people are decadent. They're not."

"Phyl, have another drink," said Gerald, holding his hand out for her glass. He grinned at her. "I'd forgotten what a girl you are for causes."

"That's what's wrong with most of us today," Phyllis said. "We haven't got a goal." Her voice was still vibrant, but she made an effort to steady it.

"You're right, of course, Mrs. Medhurst," Patrick said. "And there are plenty of industrious, well-conducted youngsters about who get pretty fed-up with their ill-disciplined contemporaries. Unfortunately the acts of the virtuous don't make news, and we're conditioned today to seek sensation. Every non-event is reported as a crisis."

They discussed this theme at some length, and then Patrick rose to go, saying that he hoped they would all come down to Reynard's one evening before he returned to Oxford.

He had walked up to Pantons. It was not very far, and after a day spent idly in the garden he thought the exercise would do him good. As he walked back down the drive he heard a car's engine start up, close at hand. He stepped off the gravel into the shelter of some shrubs, and was passed by a small, dark saloon, a Vauxhall Viva, which turned into the road at the lodge gates and with a sudden roar accelerated rapidly away.

IV

Phyllis and Cathy stayed at the Stable House for another hour after Patrick left. Cathy wanted to see Helen's photographs of Venice, and to hear again the romantic story of the meeting in the jeweller's shop; she was wearing her bracelet.

"I should love to go to Venice," said Phyllis.

"Have you never been to Italy, Phyllis?" Helen asked.

"No. I've never been over the Channel," Phyllis said. "I went to Africa during the war, to Alexandria and Cairo. I haven't been abroad since then."

"And you're so close!" Helen marvelled. "We have such distances to cover in the States, we just expect you Britishers to be always popping over to France."

"Phyl's been very tied here, with Mother," Gerald said.

"Of course. I didn't realise," said Helen. "Well, you must take a trip next year, Phyllis. I'll be able to help out with your mother, if she'll let me."

"We'll see," said Phyllis. She never planned further than a week ahead. Helen would discover that Mrs. Ludlow was a considerable force to be reckoned with, capable of upsetting the most careful plans for a whim. Luckily, however, she seemed to have taken a fancy to the newcomer, and if this lasted, things might improve all round.

"Where did you live, in America?" Cathy wanted to know.

"Oh, all over," Helen said. "I was born in Maryland. Then my parents moved to Seattle. I worked in New York for quite a while."

"What did you do?"

"I was at the U.N.," Helen said. "I was a stenographer."

"How long were you there?"

"Two years. Then I got married and went to Washington."

"That's a beautiful city, " Gerald said.

"Oh, you went there, didn't you, Daddy? When you were in America three years ago. Where were you then, Helen?"

"I wasn't in the States then," Helen said. "But I've lived in Wyoming, and in San Francisco," she added.

"Not Hollywood?"

Helen laughed.

"No, not Hollywood," she said. "And you've always lived

here, haven't you, Gerry? Apart from the war, I mean, and your schooldays?"

"And the flat in town," said Gerald.

"It must give you a safe kind of feeling," Helen said. "Here are your roots and here you belong." She looked a little wistful. It occurred to Cathy that these two must still have much to learn about each other. Her father looked different in some subtle way; younger, and vulnerable: the word came into her mind spontaneously and surprised her. She was oddly touched, and she felt benevolent towards them both.

"We must go, Cathy," said Phyllis. "It's getting late. We'll see you two for lunch tomorrow. You'll soon get used to our Sunday lunches, Helen. It's like a flash-back to Edwardian days."

"The food's super," Cathy said. "Melting beef, and fresh vegetables from the garden. Gran will only buy what can't be grown in England, like oranges and things."

"Mother is a very knowledgeable wheel-chair gardener," said Gerald. "She'll take you on a tour tomorrow, Helen."

"Well, I don't know much about flowers," said Helen. "But I do know quite a lot about vegetables."

"That's unusual," said Phyllis. "Most women know about flowers, if they're gardeners, and not about vegetables."

"I once lived in a place where we farmed vegetables," said Helen. She got up as she said this and went over to the bowl of mixed flowers that were on the window sill. "What are these called, Phyllis?" she asked, touching a bronze helenium. Phyllis told her. Altogether she had arranged three vases in the room, which contained a fair representation of late summer blooms.

"There's always plenty to pick in the garden," Phyllis said. "And Bludgen brings on chrysanthemums and so on under glass. We have our own cyclamen and azaleas."

"I can see I have a lot to learn," said Helen.

"Mother'll soon teach you," Gerald said.

"Come on, Cathy, we must go," Phyllis said again. "Thanks for the drinks, Gerald. Goodnight, both of you."

"Goodnight, old girl," said Gerald. He gave his sister a brisk kiss on the cheek, at which she looked surprised, but pleased.

"Goodnight, Daddy," Cathy said. "It's nice to have you back." She kissed him, hesitated, and then kissed Helen too, shyly, but with warmth. "He's not a bad old Dad," she said gruffly. "You're quite lucky, really."

"I think I'm very lucky, Cathy dear," said Helen. She slid her arm through Gerald's as they stood in the lighted doorway of the Stable House to watch Phyllis and Cathy departing up the drive.

"What a nice daughter you have, Gerry," she said softly, rubbing her cheek against his shoulder.

"I knew you'd like each other. What did I tell you?" Gerald said, closing the door upon the vanishing figures. "All those panic stations we had before you'd marry me! You'll do her so much good, sweetheart. She needs someone like you around. And so do I." He proceeded to demonstrate to her the truth of this remark.

Much later, as the moonlight slanted in through their open bedroom window, Helen stretched out a bare arm and gently sought Gerald's face. She touched his cheek softly, caressing it, and he caught her hand and kissed it, opening her palm and pouring little kisses into it, then closing her fingers tight around them.

"I'm frightened, Gerry," Helen said.

"You needn't be," said Gerald. "You're safe now."

SUNDAY

I

Cathy came up from the mists of sleep wondering what sound had wakened her. It went on and on, sharp and persistent. Then she realised that it was her grandmother's bell echoing through the house. Why did no one answer? She got out of bed and ran along the passage in her nightdress. The sound of the bell still pealed as Cathy knocked on Mrs. Ludlow's door and opened it.

"Where is everybody? Can no one find time to attend to a poor old lady?" demanded her grandmother in an angry voice, to the accompaniment of a thumping sound.

Cathy went in. The old lady was sitting up in bed wearing a chiffon nightcap over her short white hair, furiously working the bell-push with one hand and banging on the floor with her silver-headed stick in the other.

"What's the matter, Gran?" asked Cathy.

"Where's my breakfast? That's what I want to know," cried Mrs. Ludlow. "Look at the time, it's almost nine. I'm hungry."

At eight o'clock on weekdays and at half-past eight on Sundays, Mrs. Ludlow's tray of tea, toast and a soft-boiled egg punctually appeared in her room.

"Oh heavens!" exclaimed Cathy. What could have happened? Mrs. Mackenzie must have overslept, though she never remembered such a thing happening before. "I'll go down and see if it's ready," she said.

"You can't walk about the house like that, child. Put your dressing-gown on," ordered Mrs. Ludlow.

"All right, Gran. I won't be long," said Cathy. She hurried back to her room, put on her old blue woollen dressing-gown, then went back along the landing to the top of the stairs.

Aunt Phyllis's door was closed, but she had gone to church; she often went early on Sundays unless Grandmother had decided to make one of her increasingly rare appearances at matins. In any case, she should be back soon.

Cathy pattered lightly down the stairs in her bare feet, crossed the hall and went into the kitchen. It was empty.

"What a joke! Fancy Mrs. Mack oversleeping!" she marvelled. Well, she had better set to and make her grandmother's breakfast; there would be still more of a delay if she woke Mrs. Mack first. All the household knew well enough what Mrs. Ludlow ate. Cathy put the kettle on, and a pan for the egg. The tray was already laid with the special Crown Derby china always used for Mrs. Ludlow, and covered with a spotless cloth. While she waited for the water to boil, Cathy went into the garden and plucked a rose to put on the tray, an action she had read about in one of the novels Aunt Phyllis so much enjoyed. Under the soles of her bare feet the paved slabs of the garden path were already warm in the sun.

The kettle had begun to sing when she went back into the house. She watched the toast and timed the egg carefully; Gran would soon make a fuss if the crusts were not neatly cut, or the bread were too pale or too dark, or if her egg had been boiled too long. Soon it was all ready, and she went up with the tray, travelling in the lift this time in case she spilled the tea.

"This should be all right, Gran," she said optimistically, after she had got out the bed-table and set it across Mrs. Ludlow's knees. It was quite a business, settling her with her back-rest in position. Cathy felt sure that her aunt or Mrs. Mackenzie usually got her grandmother washed and tidied before breakfast, but this was a daunting task that she was reluctant to undertake.

"Hm, hm, let me see. What have you forgotten? Toast, egg, butter, tea. Yes, child. How long did you cook the egg?"

"Three minutes, Gran." Everyone knew that this was the time allowed.

"Very well, very well."

"Shall I take the top off for you?" Cathy offered.

"Certainly not. I'm not quite helpless yet," said Mrs. Ludlow tartly. She took up the teaspoon and cracked the egg, then peeled the pieces of shell away, exposing the quivering white.

"I always decapitate mine with a knife," Cathy volunteered,

watching her grandmother's gnarled hands at work. They were quite steady, and considering how swollen and lumpy they were, remarkably deft.

"How vulgar," said Mrs. Ludlow. "Well, why was I forgotten?"

"You weren't, Gran. But Aunt Phyl must have gone to church, and I suppose Mrs. Mackenzie's overslept. I'd better wake her up."

"Phyllis should be back by now. Let her go," said Mrs. Ludlow.

"She isn't back. I don't expect she'll be long," Cathy said.

"Well, you go and get dressed. Then come back and see if I've finished. I don't like being left with my tray."

"All right, Gran," said Cathy.

"You may pour out my tea before you go," said Mrs. Ludlow. She picked up the rose that Cathy had put on her tray and sniffed it; slowly her features bent into what was, for her, a smile, but she made no comment. Cathy poured out her tea, and as she left the room she heard her grandmother start to mutter away under her breath.

Phyllis did not get back from church until nearly half-past nine, much later than her usual time. She hurried into the house and went upstairs to take off her hat. She could hear the sound of voices from her mother's room, and hurried along the landing. Inside, she found Cathy standing by the window while Mrs. Ludlow finished her second cup of tea.

"You're late, Phyllis," said the old lady, without preamble.

"Yes, I'm sorry. The vicar delayed me. He asked me to thank you for your note, Mother, and said he'd come and see you tomorrow. He seemed overwhelmed. What did you write to him about?"

"That's my affair," said Mrs. Ludlow. "And I don't want to see him. Ring him up and tell him so. I'll send for him when I want him."

"Very well, Mother," said Phyllis. "You're a long time finishing your breakfast this morning. Was Mrs. Mackenzie late?"

"She's overslept," said Cathy, giggling. "Isn't it a hoot? I got Gran's breakfast."

"Overslept? Good heavens, she'll never have lunch ready," said Phyllis. "Go and wake her at once, Cathy."

"Don't send the child. You go, Phyllis," said Mrs. Ludlow, but Cathy had already left the room. Phyllis moved her mother's tray and folded up the table; then she began her preparations for the old lady's morning toilet.

Suddenly Cathy was back. Her face was green. Phyllis, at the dressing-table collecting brush and hand-mirror, saw her reflection in the looking-glass and turned sharply.

"Auny Phyl, can you come?" said Cathy. "Come quickly." She said no more but hurried out of the room. Phyllis put down the brush and followed at once.

"What is it? What's the matter?" she said.

Cathy made signs indicating that her grandmother should not overhear. With her hand to her mouth she led her aunt along the passage and stopped outside Mrs. Mackenzie's bedroom door.

"Mrs. Mack's ill," she said, and gulped. "I think she's dead."

II

Dr. Wilkins was luckily at home, out in the garden early, practising putting on the lawn and hoping not to be summoned away from his Sunday recreation by any emergency. He reached Pantons within fifteen minutes of Phyllis's telephone call.

She took him up to Mrs. Mackenzie's bedroom, explaining what had happened as they went, though he already knew most of it from what she had said on the telephone.

Shafts of sunlight streamed in through the window and slanted across the bed where the still figure lay as though sleeping. The bedclothes were drawn up round her shoulders and she was curled up in a defenceless position, like a child.

"It was obviously too late to do anything for her," Phyllis said. "She's been dead for several hours, hasn't she?"

The doctor bent over the body, turning it gently over on to its back. It had begun to stiffen.

"Yes," he said. He lifted an eyelid and gazed intently at the eye.

"What could it have been? A stroke?" Phyllis spoke in a hushed voice. She felt extremely shocked, and had a strange, prim thought that she should have drawn the bedroom curtains so that a muted light prevailed instead of this bright, all-revealing sunshine.

"Perhaps. It's impossible to say," said the doctor. "It could have been heart. We'll have to wait for the post-mortem to be sure."

"Oh dear! Must that happen? Can't you really tell?"

"I'm afraid not. And I haven't seen her professionally for a very long time," said the doctor. He drew the sheet up over the dead woman's face. "Mrs. Mackenzie always seemed to be in excellent health whenever I came to see your mother."

"She did. I don't even remember her having a cold," said Phyllis.

"She was rather over-weight. Otherwise I should have said she was very fit," said the doctor. "I shall have to notify the coroner."

He picked up a glass that stood on a table beside the bed and sniffed it. Then he held it to the light.

"Whisky," he said. "Did she drink much?"

"She liked a nightcap," Phyllis said. "She kept a bottle up here. Why not? It's her own room, after all."

"Why not, indeed?" agreed the doctor. He crossed to the dressing-table, where a number of bottles and jars were tidily arranged, and inspected them. They all appeared to be of a cosmetic nature. In one corner of the room was a wash-basin, and above it a small mirror-fronted cabinet. Dr. Wilkins opened this and looked inside. It contained aspirins, Enos, a bottle of Milton, and one or two other simple medicaments. On a shelf below it, Mrs. Mackenzie's dentures rested in a tumbler of water.

"She didn't take sleeping-pills?" asked the doctor.

"Not as far as I know," said Phyllis. "She slept very well, as a matter of fact. We'd discussed it, because as you know I often have to get up to Mother and I don't find it easy to go off again." That was when she did most of her reading, escaping into the company of swash-buckling Regency bucks if she could not relax.

"I've certainly never prescribed any for her," the doctor said. "But she could have got hold of some."

Phyllis looked down at the unmoving mound in the bed.

"You don't think—?" She broke off, staring at the doctor with a startled expression.

"I don't know," said the doctor. "It's a possibility. We shall have to wait for the answer. I'll telephone now and make the arrangements. Then I'd better see your mother. This will have shaken her. Have you told her?"

"Yes. She realised that something had happened, so I thought it the best thing to do. My brother's with her now. She's taken it very calmly. Cathy's much more upset; she found Mrs. Mackenzie."

"How very unfortunate," said Dr. Wilkins. "What a shock for her."

"It's a shock for us all," said Phyllis. "We were fond of her." And how would they manage without her, she began to wonder, her practical sense returning after its initial numbing.

She took the doctor downstairs to the hall to telephone, and then went into her mother's room. Gerald was sitting beside the old lady's bed.

"Well?" he asked, getting up as Phyllis came in.

Phyllis shook her head at him.

"Mother, Dr. Wilkins will be in to see you in a minute," she said. "He's just making a phone call first." She glanced round the room, and added, "Where's Cathy?"

"Helen came up. They're making some coffee," said Gerald.

"I don't need the doctor to see me," said Mrs. Ludlow crossly, cutting across his words. "I just want a little of somebody's time and attention to get me dressed."

"Yes, Mother. I'll see to you as soon as the doctor's gone," said Phyllis in soothing tones.

"What did he say? It was her heart, wasn't it?" Mrs. Ludlow demanded. "She looked as if she had a bad heart. She was too fat and too red in the face."

"The doctor isn't quite sure what happened, mother," Phyllis said. "But he thinks it probably was a heart attack." It was no good letting her mother know how vague in fact the doctor had been.

"I thought she always seemed very healthy," said Gerald. "And fresh-complexioned, not apoplectic."

Phyllis frowned at him. What use to anyone was an argument? Mrs. Mackenzie was dead; that was a fact, and it was quite enough to be going on with.

"We'll have to tell her family," she said, in a worried voice. "That son in Clapham. I don't know his address."

"It's bound to be somewhere in her room," said Gerald. "I'll go and have a hunt for it while you clear up in here."

He crossed the room to the door, and Phyllis began to tidy the papers and oddments her mother had somehow managed to strew all over her bed.

"You'll get me up," said Mrs. Ludlow firmly, brandishing

her stick. "And Cathy can take me around the garden when I'm ready. It will give her something to do."

Gerald exchanged a glance with his sister as he left the room; really, the old girl was incredible. She always made a daily inspection of the garden as soon as she came downstairs. On weekdays it was Bludgen's duty to report at the house and wheel her round each morning; she knew every plant she owned and followed its fortunes like a mother her nurslings. On Sundays Phyllis or Gerald propelled her on this progress. Nothing was ever allowed to upset her routine, except an indisposition of her own, and clearly sudden death was to be no exception. He supposed that her strict ritual gave a framework to her existence.

Frowning, Gerald went along to Mrs. Mackenzie's room. Phyllis had drawn the curtains half-way, in a compromise, so that the intrusive sun was dimmed but the room was not dark. Odd how impersonal it seemed, even though Mrs. Mackenzie had lived in it for so many years. She had very few possessions on display, not even any photographs. The furnishings were those considered appropriate by Mrs. Ludlow for her housekeeper: a high, old-fashioned bed, a bright oak wardrobe and a matching dressing-table. Phyllis had added an easy chair, some cushions and a radio, and there was an elderly television set, one that had been replaced downstairs by a more modern model. There were no books or papers to be seen, no knitting under way left out; Mrs. Mackenzie kept everything concealed from view.

Gerald hunted about. He found Mrs. Mackenzie's secret hoard of whisky in the wardrobe; and in a drawer he discovered a zipped writing case which contained some letters. Amongst them was her son's address. There was nothing for it now but to ring up the young man and break the news. Gerald went out of the room, closed the door quietly, and walked slowly downstairs wondering how best to word it.

Dr. Wilkins met him at the foot of the stairs.

"The police will be here very soon to take her away," he said.

"The police?" Gerald looked startled.

"They deal with these things," said the doctor. "Meanwhile, I wonder if you can tell me something. I made out a new prescription for your mother's sleeping pills when I was here last week. Do you know if they've been collected yet?

Could Mrs. Mackenzie have fetched them? If so, it would account for her possession of sedatives."

Gerald stared at him.

"But had she got some sleeping pills? Is that what she died of?" he asked.

"I don't know. Unfortunately, as I explained to Mrs. Medhurst, until we know the post-mortem results there is no way of telling the cause of death. It may have been due to a stroke, or a heart attack, but it may have been something else. Your sister tells me that Mrs. Mackenzie seemed perfectly well last night. I just wondered about the sleeping tablets, because these accidents can happen very easily."

"Mrs. Mackenzie wasn't the sort of person to make mistakes with drugs," said Gerald. "She knew the dose. She gave my mother her medicines if Phyllis was out."

"She'd had some whisky," said the doctor. "She might have got confused. Still, maybe this is barking completely up the wrong tree. We'll simply have to wait. Meanwhile, I'll go up and see your mother."

"She seems to be quite all right," Gerald said.

"A remarkably resilient woman," said the doctor, as he went upstairs.

Gerald watched him go. He should ring up young Mackenzie, but that could wait for ten minutes until things that mattered near at hand had been dealt with.

"Helen?" he called. "Cathy? Where have you got to?"

"We're in the kitchen, Daddy," Cathy's voice replied.

Gerald crossed the hall and went into the kitchen, where he found Cathy and Helen seated at the table. In front of each of them was an untasted cup of coffee.

"Ah, coffee, just what I want," said Gerald with bogus heartiness.

"Neither of us can drink a drop," said Cathy miserably. "I feel sick."

"I know what you need," said Gerald. He left the room, and came back with a bottle of brandy from the dining-room; into each of their cups he poured a stiff tot. "Phyl could do with some too, I'm sure. Still, we'd better leave her to finish with Wilkins."

"Poor Aunt Phyl. She hasn't had a bite," said Cathy. "At least I had some cornflakes first." She got up and poured her father a cup of coffee from the pot that was keeping hot on the stove. "Here you are, Daddy."

"Thanks." Gerald added some brandy to it. "Drink up, you two," he urged, and frowned at Helen, who picked up her cup and forced some of the coffee down. Cathy obediently followed this example, grimacing as she swallowed, but it did do her good; she felt better almost at once.

"What's going to happen, Daddy?" she asked. "Helen says that poor Mrs. Mack will have to be cut up."

"Cathy dear, I didn't put it quite like that," protested Helen.

"Well, that's what a post-mortem means," said Cathy. "Didn't she have a heart attack?"

"The doctor isn't sure. He can't tell without an examination," said Gerald. "In every case of sudden death there has to be an inquiry, unless the person has been seen recently by a doctor and the death can be explained."

"It's awful," Cathy shivered. "There she was last night, as cheerful as could be. Why, she spent hours yesterday making a charlotte russe for today's lunch. She made a special little one for herself, too, in case we didn't leave her any, and she loves it. Used to, I mean." At this, she suddenly burst into tears and Gerald put his arm round her.

"There, there, little one," he said, trying to think of words to comfort her. "She can't have suffered. She was lying very peacefully, just as if she was asleep."

"I know," wailed Cathy. "I thought she was asleep. But she was icy, icy cold!"

III

Hardly to his surprise, for his patient's tough constitution had long been known to him, Dr. Wilkins found Mrs. Ludlow in good order. However, he advised a quiet day and an early night.

"I had dinner in bed last night," she told him. "I never keep late hours, as you are aware, but we had such an excitement on Friday. My son Gerald brought home his bride. You'll meet her when you go downstairs."

"Indeed?" said the doctor, shutting up his bag. "I didn't know Mr. Ludlow was planning to re-marry."

"It was quite a surprise to us all," said Mrs. Ludlow. "She's

an American, quite charming. The family is delighted." This
was uttered in regal tones.

"Splendid, splendid," said the doctor, his mind already on
what else must now be done. It would be as well if the old
lady were to be diverted while the body was removed; this
could not be managed without some disturbance in the house,
so someone must distract her during the operation.

"I'll come down with you, Dr. Wilkins," said Phyllis, who
was in the room with them. "I won't be long, Mother."

"Send Helen up," ordered Mrs. Ludlow. "She can help me
with my hair. She may as well learn what I need done."

It was true. Until a replacement for Mrs. Mackenzie could
be found, Helen might be very useful, if she were willing.
Betty's help was of doubtful value, for she was so clumsy that
she was bound to pull Mrs. Ludlow's hair or bang into the
furniture and bump the bed, however anxious she was to
lend assistance.

Phyllis felt gloomy about the future as she led the way out
of her mother's room.

"Come and have some coffee, Phyl. You must need it,"
Gerald said, appearing in the kitchen doorway when he heard
her and the doctor coming downstairs. "You too, Dr. Wilkins. I've got some brandy here as well."

"Just the medicine," said the doctor.

"Helen, Mother wants you to go and help her with her
hair," said Phyllis. "Could you bear it?"

"I'll go," said Gerald.

"She wants Helen," Phyllis said.

"Of course I'll go," said Helen, standing up, a neat figure
in her dark linen dress.

"I'll come too, shall I?" offered Cathy.

"No, you stay where you are, my dear, and let your coffee
settle," said Helen. "Your grandmother won't eat me. You
forget that I'm used to elderly ladies."

"Phew, well, this will be a baptism of fire," said Cathy,
with a wry look.

"Grandmother wants you to take her round the garden,
Cathy," said Phyllis. "I should hang on till then, if I were
you, as long as Helen doesn't mind."

Thumping sounds and the pealing of a bell could now be
heard as Mrs. Ludlow declared her impatience. Helen laid
her hand lightly on Gerald's arm for an instant, and then she
left the room.

The others sat down round the table again, and Cathy poured out the coffee for her aunt and the doctor. Gerald added generous amounts of brandy, and after they had sipped meditatively for a minute or two, Dr. Wilkins spoke.

"Mrs. Medhurst, I gave you a new prescription for your mother's sodium amytal capsules last week. Have they been collected yet?"

Phyllis looked surprised. She exchanged a glance with her brother.

"I got them from Fennersham on Friday," she said. "But Mrs. Mackenzie couldn't have taken any of them, if that's what you're thinking. They're still in the chemist's parcel in the hall, where I left them. I was rather rushed on Friday and forgot to put them away, as I normally do at once. Mother still had a few left from the previous lot, in her room."

"You're sure the new ones are still in the hall?"

"Quite sure. I noticed them this morning. The car keys are kept on the chest in the hall, and the pills were there when I went to church. I remember thinking that I should have put them away."

Dr. Wilkins got up and went out into the hall. He came back carrying a small paper bag printed with the name of the Fennersham chemist.

"It's a pity chemists don't still seal their packets up with wax, as they used to do," he said, opening the bag.

He took the bottle out.

There was no need to say anything. The three who watched could see for themselves that the bottle was half-empty.

IV

"And what happened after that?" demanded Patrick.

It was the same afternoon. Cathy was sitting with him and Jane in the living-room at Reynard's relating the events of the morning. At intervals in her tale Patrick had stopped her, making her clarify what she had said and ensuring that she left out no detail.

"Oh, Patrick, stop it. Leave her alone, for heaven's sake," said Jane. "Poor girl, it's been an awful experience for her."

"It's much better for her to get it all off her chest rather than bottle it up," Patrick said.

"I hate you, Patrick Grant," said his sister. "Your ordinary curiosity is bad enough, but this is too much. Forget it, Cathy."

"I can't, Jane. Don't you see, I keep going over and over it all in my mind as it is," Cathy said. "I'm only telling you what I've already told the police. How can any of us think of anything else for a single minute? Even when we know why she did it, it will haunt us for ever. She must have been so unhappy, to do something so terrible, yet she always seemed cheerful." She shook her head in bewilderment. "I just don't understand it. She'd got a nice son and daughter, and grandchildren, and we were all fond of her. Besides, there was the charlotte russe."

"What about it?"

"Mrs. Mack had made a little one for herself, for lunch today, as well as a big one for us. She would never have done that if she hadn't intended to eat it," she said.

There was a silence.

"I'm inclined to believe you," Patrick said.

"Then there was all that about the lemon meringue," Cathy went on. "Oh, I don't see what it means."

"What about the lemon meringue?"

"We had it for supper last night. The police asked about it. We had cold cucumber soup, and chicken fricassee, and then lemon meringue pie. Gran had hers in bed, she often does, but last night she didn't eat her pudding. She said she was full. It's unusual, because she has a very good appetite. Maybe that was why she was so starving this morning, at breakfast-time."

"Let me get this straight," Patrick said. "Your grandmother didn't eat her pudding last night, right?"

"Right. She'd had rather a lot of excitement the night before, with Father and Helen arriving, so I suppose it wasn't all that surprising, but it's one of her favourite puddings."

"Well? And so?" Patrick prompted her.

"We couldn't find the piece. I mean, Aunt Phyl cut the pie into four, a piece each for her, Gran, Mrs. Mack and me. As Gran didn't eat hers, it should have been somewhere about, in the fridge or in the larder."

"Could it have been thrown away?"

"We looked in the bin."

"Is there a waste disposer? It might have been thrown away like that."

"Not in Winterswick," said Jane. "There's no main drainage here."

"Well, where do you think it went?" asked Patrick.

"Into Mrs. Mack, of course," said Cathy. "She'd have gobbled it up. She loved sweet things, they were her weakness. She couldn't resist eating up any left-over bits and pieces. Everyone knew that."

"Everyone?"

"Well, all the family. Everyone at Pantons. Why, Daddy mentioned it the moment he got home. He said she'd put on weight and she must have been eating too many sweets."

"Did you tell the Inspector this?"

Cathy thought for a minute.

"No. I don't think I did," she said. "In fact, I know I didn't. But it didn't arise in our conversation. Should I have?"

"It was for him to discover," said Patrick in dulce tones, and his sister gave him a look. "He will, if it matters. It was the Inspector who was looking for the pudding, was it?"

"Yes. There was a sergeant, too, in the kitchen. I'd got the dishwasher full of things, Gran's breakfast, and our cups— we'd all been drinking coffee full of brandy. They wouldn't let me switch it on. There were one or two other things in it, too, that Mrs. Mack had left."

"Such as the plate that had held the missing pie, for instance?"

"One that could have been it, yes. And a glass. Nothing else. Mrs. Mack always did the dinner things straight away," said Cathy.

"And she posted a letter yesterday morning in time to catch the mid-day clearance," Patrick said. "An extra letter to her daughter."

"That's guessing," said Jane.

"It's an informed guess," said Patrick. "It's a break from routine. If anything had upset her, the letter might say what it was."

"But she wasn't upset, Dr. Grant," Cathy insisted. "Oh, what do you think went wrong?"

"I don't know, Cathy. I just don't know," said Patrick, but he looked extremely thoughtful.

"Why don't you try and think about something more cheerful, Cathy?" said Jane. "Your university entrance, for instance."

"I can't really think about it now," Cathy sighed. She made an effort, and added, "I suppose I should aim high and start with a bash at Oxford."

"Indeed you should. How about writing to the principal of St. Joan's and putting out feelers? I'll write too, and say you seem a promising wench," said Patrick.

"Oh, would you? Do you know her?"

"Intimately," said Patrick with a grin. "She's my aunt."

After Cathy had gone, which she did in a sudden rush, saying she must go and help with the chores, Jane gave Patrick another severe scolding.

"Say what you like, it did the girl good to spill it out," he repeated. "And she has a well-ordered mind, too. She told it well."

"Who cares about how she told it? Poor child, she comes down here to escape for half-an-hour, and you pin her down like a butterfly on a board with your beastly questions."

"How colourfully you express yourself, Jane," he said admiringly. "A fine turn of phrase, that, about the butterfly."

"Oh, you're a brute, an insensitive brute," said Jane.

"And pretty, too, when roused," Patrick went on.

"Swine," said Jane, turning on her heel. "I'm going to talk to Andrew. He at least is civilised."

"A matter of opinion, I should say," observed the baby's uncle to her departing back.

She returned some time later in a calmer mood and picked up *The Sunday Times*. Patrick had already finished the crossword, so she flung it down again with an angry mutter.

"Why are you so interested, anyway?" she demanded. "Mrs. Mackenzie's death must have been an accident."

"Yes. But what sort of accident, that's the question. Mrs. Ludlow didn't eat her lemon pie, but Mrs. Mackenzie did. Mrs. Mackenzie was loved by all, and needed; Mrs. Ludlow wasn't."

"No, Patrick. You're being sensational. You know too many thriller-writing dons," said Jane. "This is a very serious affair."

"I quite agree," said Patrick. "And justice must be done. Work it out for yourself. Mrs. Ludlow leads them all a dance, we know that. She has Phyllis Medhurst on a string, without a life of her own, and they all have to jump to it when the old girl whistles."

"Yes, but to murder her! That's what you're getting at, isn't it? The sleeping pills were in the pie and the wrong person ate it?"

"That's how it looks," said Patrick.

"But why? Lots of people have tiresome relations, but they don't bump them off."

"There must have been powerful reasons," Patrick said. "Things we don't yet know about. People are seldom only what they seem, as you should know, Jane. Behind the façades of these prim villas and gentrified cottages here in Winterswick many a drama must go on."

"No, Patrick. People are basically decent."

"Except when being decent interferes with what they want. Then they become ruthless."

"No. Only some of them."

"And murder only happens sometimes," Patrick said. "Most people cope in some fashion or other with the various strains under which they live, or they simply come out in spots, or leave home, or get drunk. But occasionally you get pressures that cause a person to snap. Then the unpredictable happens."

"But even if Mrs. Ludlow is an infuriating old woman, you're suggesting that a member of her family hated her enough to murder her."

"Hated her enough, or would profit by her death enough to want to hasten it."

"But which of them?"

"You tell me."

"Well, Phyllis could have got at the pie. No one else. Only she was at the house, last night, apart from Cathy. I presume you exempt her?"

Patrick nodded. "A decision of the emotions, not the intellect," he said.

"Emotions! You have none," said his sister. "No, I won't subscribe to this idea, Patrick. The post-mortem will show that Mrs. Mackenzie had a stroke, or her daughter will say she had some secret worry which unbalanced her. Or the chemist may have made a mistake and put up too few pills. You'll see, there will be a rational explanation. And meanwhile you've frightened Cathy off. Didn't you notice how suddenly she fled?"

"I didn't scare her away," Patrick said. "Her cousin Tim enticed her."

"What do you mean?"

"He walked past while we were talking. Cathy happened to

look out of the window and she saw him. I did too. He never looked towards the house—you don't know him, do you, Jane?"

"No."

"I recognised him all right, shaggy hair and all," said Patrick.

"How nice of him to come over to see Cathy," said Jane.

"Darling Jane, how you do believe the best of people," Patrick said. "He didn't come to cheer up Cathy, if that's what you're thinking. He came to look for this,'" and he took an envelope out of his pocket.

"What is it?"

"A letter addressed to Mr. Timothy Ludlow, St. Mark's College, Oxford," Patrick said. "I found it on the gravel outside Pantons last night, where our young friend must have dropped it earlier in the evening." He tapped the envelope and gave her a sardonic look. "Well? Aren't you going to ask me if I've read it?"

"I'm bloody sure you have," said Jane sourly.

"You're right," Patrick admitted. "And rather a tiresome letter it is too, in the nature of an ultimatum. It's just as well I found it, not the police. The young idiot's got to find a lot of money rather quickly."

"So he went to ask his rich old granny for some. Bully for him. Very wise," said Jane.

"But what if granny said no?"

"But you can't mean that Tim—a boy of twenty . . .?" Jane's voice trailed away.

"I trust sincerely not," said Patrick. "But this shows you what I mean, Jane. The Ludlows, like everybody else, have their secrets. By chance I've found out Tim's. What about the rest of them? Phyllis has one, we know that too, by another chance. But there are the brothers. Derek may have something he wants to hide; so may his wife. Then there's Gerald, the happy bridegroom; what about him? Past mistresses, perhaps? And Timothy's brother, who seems to have left the family fold? We don't know anything much about him. And who visited Pantons last night in a Vauxhall Viva whose number I managed to make out as it passed me in the drive?"

Jane stared at her brother. She looked frightened.

"I don't like this, Patrick," she said. "I don't like this theorising."

"It isn't all theory. Some of this is fact," Patrick said. "And only facts will do."

"Are you going to give that letter to the police?"

"Not yet. Officially, we only know that Mrs. Mackenzie has unfortunately died." He paused. "We'll see what happens at the inquest. By that time I may have found out some other secrets, enough to show me who has one important enough to yield a motive for murder."

MONDAY

I

Betty Ludlow had moved from the shrubbery to the herba-
ceous border. There were still vivid patches of colour in it,
where Michaelmas daisies and coreopsis bloomed, and huge-
faced daisies like giant sun-flowers; but there were other,
withered shoots to be cut down, and it was not too soon to
start forking over the earth in readiness for winter. Across an
area where only paeonies and lupins were supposed to be, a
rapid-spreading artemesia straggled, strangling weaker plants,
and she attacked it fiercely; it would soon reappear as strongly
as before.

For a time, while she toiled, she thought of nothing but
the work in hand. Her square figure bent and straightened,
bent and straightened, as she turned the soil, creating order
where there had been confusion. Presently, however, her
mind harked back to the day before. What a dreadful Sunday
it had been.

She had been busy in the kitchen when Gerald telephoned
with the news from Pantons. Derek was already in his study,
poring over some papers he had brought back from the office,
and not pleased at being interrupted, but when he heard the
reason he drove over to his mother's house at once. He soon
returned, though, saying that nothing could be done. Alec
Mackenzie had been told and was coming down by train.
Gerald and the police between them would deal with him.

Betty could not understand why the police were concerned.
Something about sleeping pills and whisky, it seemed, but
there must be some mistake. Mrs. Mackenzie was in no way
morbid; she would never have killed herself. Her son had
said so too, evidently.

53

It was the first time they had ever missed Sunday lunch at Pantons, except when they were away from home, and that was rarely. Betty had broached her freezer for a stew, and she, Derek and Tim had sat round the dining-table in glum silence, trying to assume an appetite none had. Soon Tim had risen, and flounced out of the house with a toss of his long, shaggy hair, saying he was going away. She and Derek, left alone, had decided that Mrs. Mackenzie had had a seizure and the chemist must have put up only half the prescription ordered; this was the only possible explanation.

In the evening they had telephoned Martin to let him know what had happened. At first there was no reply from the Chelsea house; it was after eleven o'clock when Martin and Sandra returned from wherever they had been and heard the news.

Betty dug doggedly on, remembering all this. Derek had scarcely slept all night. For weeks now he had been wakeful; it was most unlike him, for normally he slumbered like a basking seal, occasionally snoring, for seven hours at least, while she lay restless, her mind darting about worrying over Tim and his long, greasy hair and failed exams. Sometimes, for a change, she agonised about Martin instead, puzzling over his relationship with his wife, who seemed so implacably cool and detached; impossible to imagine Sandra pregnant, or even, in the act of love, dishevelled. With such nocturnal reflections Betty shocked and alarmed herself, forgetting that few parents understood their children. She lay wooing sleep by various means, like going through the alphabet reciting to herself the names of plants, beginning with Anchusa and so on down, by way of Mignonette, at last to Zinnia. Then she would try shrubs, starting with Azalea, and cheating sometimes, for they were harder, and finally on to fruit and vegetables, often enough, before sleep came at last. All this time, as a rule, Derek would be solidly beside her, a large, gently pulsating hump, comforting merely by his presence.

But recently, as she lay staring at the ceiling, or at the patch of paler darkness where the window was, or at coloured patterns shooting across the blackness of her tightly shut eyes, she had known that he was not sleeping either. He would lie unnaturally still, feigning the even breath of slumber, unwilling to acknowledge that he was disturbed, and for the first time in their long marriage inhibiting her. Was it a business worry, or was it worse: some other woman?

Last night they both had a clear-cut reason for their sleeplessness, and the invisible barrier that had grown up between them in the past few weeks had been dissolved. They lay awake, talking about Mrs. Mackenzie and about their boys for quite a time. This was a consolation.

Betty gently eased a clump of iris up, so that the rhizomes showed above the ground. As she bent to her work again, a large black police car turned in at the gate and drove slowly up to the front door.

II

"I hate leaving you to all this on your own, darling," Gerald said. He stood in the hall of the Stable House with his arms round Helen. "I wish I could stay with you."

"So do I, but there it is," said Helen. She gave him a quick kiss. "Don't worry. There's plenty to do. All our unpacking, for a start, and Phyllis may like some help during the day. Then there's Cathy. Maybe she could show me the village this afternoon, if she's not too busy."

"That's a good idea," said Gerald. It would do both of them good to get away from the atmosphere up at Pantons for a time. Gerald let her go and picked up his briefcase. "I'll be back as early as I can make it, sweetheart, but I've been away from the office for so long that there are things I must attend to. And I'm sure to have to take more time off before this business is finally cleared up. I must be here for the inquest, at least."

"I know, dear," Helen said.

"After everything that's happened, to think there should be this to face now," said Gerald bitterly.

"I keep telling you not to worry," Helen said. She kissed him again. "Soon we shall forget it all."

"Yes. Oh, damn it all to hell," Gerald said. He put his brief-case down again and caught her to him once more. "I wanted to make up to you for everything," he told her.

"You do, darling. You have, and you will," she insisted.

He started to kiss her again, until at last she broke away from him.

"Darling, you must go," she said gently.

But when he had gone, she felt alone and afraid. She

occupied herself for a time by clearing away the breakfast dishes and making a list of stores that she must get. Perhaps there was a grocery in Winterswick where she could buy them. She had just found the vacuum sweeper, stowed away in a closet under the stairs, when there was a contrived cough in the background and she looked up to see a small woman with bright red hair standing in the hall.

Helen's heart thumped. Ridiculous to be so terrified.

"Beg pardon, Mrs. Ludlow, if I startled you. I'm Mrs. Bludgen, come to clean," said the stranger.

The pounding in Helen's temples slowed. Mrs. Bludgen from the lodge. Phyllis had said something about a woman to help with the housework, but that had been on Friday night: so long ago, it seemed.

"Oh, good morning, Mrs. Bludgen. I hadn't realised you'd be here today," said Helen, speaking calmly.

"Mondays and Thursdays are my days," Mrs. Bludgen said. "I oblige Mrs. Medhurst on the other mornings. I'll just take that sweeper, madam, if you please." She reached out for the cleaner.

Helen surrendered it.

"All right, Mrs. Bludgen. You'd better carry on," she said faintly. This was an example of that formidable person she had read about in novels and seen portrayed in British movies, the daily help. Phyllis would have to explain how she should be managed, if indeed she must be kept at all.

"What a terrible thing about poor Mrs. Mackenzie," Mrs. Bludgen eagerly remarked, whilst at the same time in one movement somehow plugging in the sweeper and removing her own mock suède jacket. "I said to Bludgen, you could have knocked me down with a feather when I heard. I was talking to her on Saturday, as large as life; stopped by, she did, to pass the time of day on her way back from the village. And now she's dead. It makes you think."

"It's very sad," said Helen.

"Of course, you didn't know her, Mrs. Ludlow," said Mrs. Bludgen, disappearing into the cupboard and coming out again with tins of polish and a pile of dusters. "But she was quite a nice person. What her boy will do I don't know."

"Her boy?"

"Her son in London. Young Alec. Devoted, he was. Ah, dear," Mrs. Bludgen sighed. She began to rub polish into the hall table. Helen ironically wondered if she put as much effort into her work when there was no witness.

"And the police are up at the house just now," Mrs. Bludgen added. In fact, she had thought Phyllis might require her assistance more than the new Mrs. Ludlow today, in view of what had happened; and curious though she was to get a sight of the American lady, events at the big house were much more compelling. So she had felt snubbed when turned away at the door first by a policeman, and then by Phyllis herself.

Helen stiffened. It was unlikely that anyone outside the family knew many details yet; better keep it so for as long as possible.

"It's usual, when there's been a sudden death," she said firmly.

"Oh, I know," said Mrs. Bludgen, who saw such things all the time on television. "I expect she had a heart attack, poor soul."

"I expect she did," Helen agreed.

The longer everyone in Winterswick thought the same, the better. The moment a hint of anything else escaped, down would come the Press, like vultures on the scene, and who knew what might happen then, what past embarrassments for everyone might be resurrected? Helen knew the power of newspapers.

She murmured something and went upstairs, leaving Mrs. Bludgen to her speculations.

Mrs. Bludgen polished on, more lingeringly now, musing. There was much to think about, for once. Usually there was only old Mrs. Ludlow's latest tantrum to dominate the scene, but now there were alternatives, Mr. Gerald's new wife, for instance. She seemed a frail little thing. Still, it was time he got married; he should have done it years ago, for Cathy's sake, if not his own. Mrs. Medhurst did her best, but it wasn't right for the girl to be cooped up in that big house with a bad-tempered old witch and a frustrated aunt. Oh, Mrs. Medhurst might have been married once, but it was only in name, Mrs. Bludgen was convinced. She too read lurid novels. Mrs. Medhurst was often touchy and awkward, though, to be fair, she was just. Still, she was a disappointed woman, that was certain.

And now, on top of Mr. Gerald's wedding, there had come a sudden death. It went to show, thought Mrs. Bludgen, who had seen something sinister in her tea-cup only last Wednesday, drinking her elevenses in the kitchen up at Pantons, and had said as much to Joyce Mackenzie. She plugged in the sweeper. Joyce had not reacted. She was always one to keep her distance; thought herself superior, Mrs. Bludgen had often said to Bludgen, and much good it had done her now. But sad and shocking as it was, you couldn't deny that things like this took you out of yourself. Two, there'd been: the wedding, and the death. There was bound to be a third.

She pushed the cleaner back and forth across the carpet. Helen, upstairs in her bedroom, heard the sound it made as she sat before the mirror at her dressing-table, staring at her own white and frightened face.

III

Inspector Foster was well accustomed to hostility, and recognised it at once as personified by Phyllis Medhurst, who had not looked pleased at finding him and Sergeant Smithers upon the doorstep of Pantons that Monday morning.

"Just one or two queries, Mrs. Medhurst, about your movements on Saturday evening," the Inspector said, when with obvious reluctance she had let him in.

"I've already told you what we all did," Phyllis said.

"I want to check it with you," said the Inspector. He still hoped the business might be sorted out before the inquest, which had been arranged for the following morning. By that time the forensic boys should have produced the expected confirmation that death was due to excess of barbiturate; it would be gratifying if he could by then present the coroner with an account of how it came to be administered, but at the moment it seemed unlikely under the complicated circumstances.

"You'd better come in here," said Phyllis, leading the way into the study, a room that was seldom used, and where her father's guns and books on country lore were still kept. Sometimes her mother demanded to be wheeled in here, and would sit alone, brooding, for an hour or more. Here, too, at her father's desk, Phyllis prepared the household accounts, verified the bills, and wrote the cheques out ready for her mother's signature.

She sat down in the swivel chair before that desk; she was not going to let the Inspector use it. Perforce, he lowered himself into a sagging leather chair and motioned to the red-haired Sergeant to find another seat.

"Now then," Inspector Foster said. He took out a notebook and consulted it. "You last saw Mrs. Mackenzie alive on Saturday evening. At what time?"

"At about eight-fifteen. My niece and I left the house then to spend the evening with my brother. I've told you," Phyllis said.

"What was Mrs. Mackenzie doing when you saw her?" asked the Inspector, ignoring this bad temper.

"She was finishing her meal. I put my head round the kitchen door and told her we were off."

"I see. And when did you return?"

"It was getting on for half-past ten."

"Mrs. Mackenzie had gone to bed?"

"Yes. At least, she was in her room. I don't know if she was in bed. She'd settled my mother down earlier."

"She had a television set in her room. It was not on?"

"I've no idea. I didn't stand outside her door, listening," said Phyllis caustically. "Her room is at the far end of the corridor from mine."

"You saw no light?"

"I didn't look. Her window is at the back of the house and I wouldn't have noticed," Phyllis said. Really, what a waste of time this was. He had heard it all before, the previous day, when he had taken statements from them all. Her mother was still not dressed and ready for the day; it would have been better to have accepted Mrs. Bludgen's well-meant offer of help with all the extra work, but she had a prying eye and Phyllis did not want her in the house until the puzzle was resolved, a view the Inspector seemed to share, though he had left the final decision to her.

"And yesterday you went to church? At what time?"

"I left the house at twenty minutes to eight," Phyllis said.

"And the sodium amytal capsules were on the hall chest then? You did not open the bottle?"

"No. There were still three left in the previous one. I had meant to take the new ones upstairs, but what with my brother's arrival and one thing and another, I forgot," Phyllis said. "It was careless, I admit. But we are used to having drugs about; my mother has pills for her heart, and for other purposes. There aren't any children here who might take them by mistake."

"Tell me what happened when you got back from church," said the Inspector. "The time first."

"It was twenty-five past nine. I was very late," Phyllis said.

"Why was that?"

"The vicar detained me. He had a message for my mother." It was true, but she had talked to someone else too, for to her amazement Maurice had been among the scanty congregation, but this was no one's business but her own.

"What did you do when you got in?"

"I went upstairs to take off my hat. Cathy was with my mother. There was no sign of Mrs. Mackenzie," Phyllis said.

"What did you think had happened?"

"I agreed with Cathy that she must have overslept. She was never ill," said Phyllis.

"Did it surprise you? Had she overslept before?"

"No. But people do oversleep," Phyllis said tartly.

"Did you know that Mrs. Mackenzie liked a nightcap on retiring?"

"Certainly I knew."

"It would not surprise you if she had several whiskies?"

"Not at all. I often have several myself. But if you mean she drank, and I assumed yesterday that she had a hangover, you're wrong," said Phyllis.

"Anyway, you sent your niece to wake her?"

"Unfortunately, yes."

"I see. Well, Mrs. Medhurst, we'll get your statement typed, and then we'll ask you to sign it, if you don't mind. Now I should like to see Mrs. Ludlow, please, and your niece," said the Inspector.

"Is that really necessary? Must you distress my mother? This has been an awful shock to her; to all of us, in fact. She can't help you."

"She was probably the last person to see Mrs. Mackenzie alive," said the Inspector. "I'm sorry, but I must insist. I did as you asked yesterday, and did not trouble her, to give her time to recover, but I must see her today."

"It's not convenient. She isn't dressed yet."

"But she's coming down?"

"Of course, when she's ready."

"Then I'll wait," said the Inspector. "And in the meanwhile, please, I'll see your niece."

"Oh, very well." It was clearly useless to protest. Phyllis gave in, with ill grace. "I'll send Cathy to you," she said, and left the room.

When Cathy came, the Inspector had moved from the low leather chair to the seat by the desk. He was a short man with a pallid face and a small, grizzled moustache; not a very inspiring figure, she thought.

"Ah, good morning, Miss Ludlow," he began, much gratifying Cathy by awarding her this adult mode of address.

As he had done with Phyllis, he checked Cathy's account of what had happened on Saturday night and on Sunday morning against what she had already told him.

"And you didn't move anything in Mrs. Mackenzie's room?"

"No. I touched her, to shake her, you know," Cathy said. "She seemed to be sleeping so heavily and did not answer me. I called her, of course, to begin with. Then I put my hand on her shoulder." She could feel again the horror of the moment. "I knew at once," she said.

"It must have been a shock for you," said the Inspector, who had a daughter of his own.

"It was," said Cathy.

There was nothing much that she could add in the way of enlightenment. She was more vague about the time she and Phyllis left the house and returned, on Saturday evening, than her aunt had been, but she confirmed her Sunday timings.

"Gran kept on so about what time it was, that's why I'm sure," she said.

"Your aunt was normally back from church sooner?"

"Yes, but she had this chat with the vicar," Cathy said. "He's a bit of an old windbag, you know. And I expect she talked to some other people too. It can be quite social in the churchyard after the service, depending on who's there. Aunt Phyl would be thinking that Mrs. Mack had everything under control here, because she always did."

"How's your grandmother taking all this?" asked the Inspector, closing his book.

"Very well. Better than any of the rest of us," Cathy said. "She's tough. I suppose she's seen so much sadness in her life that she's hardened to it."

"I'm waiting to see her now," said the Inspector. "I understand from your aunt that she isn't prepared yet for the day."

"She doesn't usually come down till ten. Then she goes

round the garden, right away, unless it's pouring. If it's drizzling, she goes round under oilskins and an umbrella. She'll be livid if you delay her," Cathy said. "Must you bother her, Inspector? Can't Aunt Phyl and I tell you what you want to know?"

"You've been very helpful, Miss Ludlow. But I must see your grandmother, I'm afraid. I'll not harass her."

"I suppose it can't be helped," said Cathy. She stood up. "Is that all? If you'll excuse me, I'll go, then. There's an awful lot to do."

"That's quite all right," said the Inspector. "I'll just wait here for your grandmother."

"You'd like some coffee, wouldn't you? I'll make some for you both," Cathy said, with a smile for the young Sergeant, who became instantly less self-effacing and beamed at her.

"That would be very agreeable," said the Inspector primly. "Smithers, go with the young lady and save her the trouble of bringing it out to us."

He gave the young man a meaning look. In chat over the kettle Cathy might let fall some casual comment of a revealing nature. To have produced a situation of this kind, Pantons must be a house full of festering hate.

Mrs. Ludlow kept him waiting some time. He and Smithers had finished their coffee and ginger nuts, and the Sergeant had removed the cups and washed them up for Cathy, who was preparing the vegetables for lunch and seemed to have done the family washing too, judging by the evidence around. Inspector Foster spent some time studying the library of the late Mr. Ludlow and the sporting prints on the walls, before the widow appeared.

He heard the faint hum that the lift made as it brought her down, and then the swishing sound of the wheelchair on the linoleum that covered the kitchen passage. Smithers opened the study door as wide as possible to admit her, and the Inspector, seated in the swivel chair, swung it round so that he faced Mrs. Ludlow as she came into the room, propelled by Phyllis.

She was dressed in some soft blue woollen garment against which her skin looked pink, and her short, cropped hair very white. Over her knees was draped a mohair rug in shades of pink and mauve, and between them she held, clasped upright, a silver-headed stick. She glowered at the Inspector, who hastily stood up, to loom above her tiny figure.

"What is all this nonsense?" she demanded, before he had time to utter.

"Good morning, madam. I am sorry to bother you, but it is my duty to make certain inquiries into matters concerning the death of Mrs. Joyce Mackenzie," he said portentously.

"The matter is perfectly plain. She had a heart attack," said Mrs. Ludlow.

"Very probably," agreed the Inspector. It would not help to complicate things at this stage. He sat down again, anxious to diminish the angle of the fierce glare burning up at him from Mrs. Ludlow's eye-level to his own.

"Leave us, Phyllis," commanded Mrs. Ludlow.

"Oh Mother, is that wise?" Phyllis asked.

"Leave us, I said," Mrs. Ludlow repeated. "Tell Bludgen to wait." For by now the gardener would have reported at the kitchen door, ready to take her round the garden.

Phyllis went from the room, and Mrs. Ludlow subjected the Inspector to a discomfiting scrutiny. He was in some imcomprehensible manner compelled to remain silent while it lasted. Finally she opened the discussion.

"Inspector, that is my late husband's chair," she said. "Kindly vacate it."

The Inspector stood up as suddenly as if he had been shot from a gun. Smithers sprang up too, and surrendered his own chair immediately, so that the Inspector ended by facing Mrs. Ludlow on a hard upright seat with his notebook awkwardly balanced on his knee. The Sergeant retreated into a corner by the wall; it would not do for either of them to sink into the recesses of the leather armchair in the presence of this formidable person.

"I apologise, madam, if I have caused offence," the Inspector managed to remark.

Mrs. Ludlow inclined her head. She sat composed.

"Well?" she said.

Inspector Foster cleared his throat.

"On Saturday night, madam, you were alone in the house with Mrs. Mackenzie, as Mrs. Medhurst and Miss Ludlow had gone down to the Stable House," he said.

"That is correct."

"According to Mrs. Medhurst, you had dinner in your room. When she and the young lady left you had not finished your meal?"

"Quite right. They rushed out. Asking for digestive trouble," Mrs. Ludlow said.

"Mrs. Mackenzie removed your tray? When was that?"

"At half-past eight precisely," Mrs. Ludlow said. "I know, because I had just turned on my wireless to listen to the play. Saturday night theatre, you know."

"Ah yes. What did you have for your meal, madam? Can you remember?"

"Of course I can remember. I'm not in my dotage, young man," snapped Mrs. Ludlow. "I had cold cucumber soup, chicken fricassee with rice and runner beans—from the garden, the only way. We eat none of your processed foodstuffs here."

"Quite so. And for sweet?"

"The pudding was lemon meringue pie. I did not eat it," Mrs. Ludlow said.

"Why was that? Don't you care for it?"

"I would not be served with a pudding I do not care for in my own house," said Mrs. Ludlow repressively. "But I was not as well as usual, that evening. I had had a tiring time the night before, greeting my new daughter-in-law."

"I'm sorry you should have this shock to face now," said the Inspector.

"So am I," said Mrs. Ludlow. "But nevertheless I shall manage to do it. My generation has more mettle than yours," she added, regarding the Inspector with disfavour.

"How did Mrs. Mackenzie seem when she removed your tray?"

"Perfectly well. We did not converse, as I was listening to the wireless."

"And was that the last time you saw her?"

"No. She brought me a glass of hot milk—I always have one at night—and assisted me to prepare finally for bed at the conclusion of the play," said Mrs. Ludlow.

"Her manner was in no way strange?"

Mrs. Ludlow frowned.

"She had been drinking," she said. "I could smell the whisky on her breath. But there was nothing amiss with her deportment."

"Did these final preparations of yours take long?"

"Five minutes or so," said Mrs. Ludlow, primping her lips. No policeman of whatever rank would extract more details from her.

"And did Mrs. Mackenzie retire to bed after that?"

"I presume so."

"What about yourself, madam?"

"I listened to the wireless for some time. I heard my daughter and my granddaughter return. My daughter saw that my light was on and she came in to make sure that I was comfortable," said Mrs. Ludlow.

"And you had a good night's sleep?"

"As good as I can hope for nowadays."

"I see. In fact, the routine that evening was quite normal?"

"Perfectly. My daughter seldom goes out, she knows her duty to her mother, but if she does, Mrs. Mackenzie has always been a satisfactory substitute."

"You'll miss her," stated the Inspector.

Mrs. Ludlow bowed her head again.

"And yesterday morning? Was that normal too?"

"You must already be aware, young man, that it was not," said Mrs. Ludlow frostily. "My breakfast was late. My granddaughter and I concluded that Mrs. Mackenzie must have overslept."

"You knew that Mrs. Medhurst had gone to church?"

"She mentioned it the night before." Mrs. Ludlow had forgotten this by morning, but there was no point in revealing her small failure to the policeman.

"So your granddaughter went to rouse Mrs. Mackenzie?"

"Phyllis should have gone herself. I told her to."

"Mrs. Ludlow, forgive this personal note, but I take it that you are on good terms with your family?"

"What an extraordinary question," exclaimed the old lady.

The Inspector searched unhappily for better phrasing.

"You approved of your son's marriage?" he hazarded.

"Why not? He's old enough to know what he is doing, I should hope. And what has this to do with Mrs. Mackenzie?"

It was no good. He would have to get at this angle from the other side; no useful purpose would be served if Mrs. Ludlow learned about the missing pills and guessed the pie had been intended for another victim. He retreated.

"I won't detain you any longer, madam," he said, putting away his notebook. "I'm sorry to have interrupted your morning."

"I should think so too," Mrs. Ludlow said. She added, more tolerantly, "I expect you have your forms to fill. It's all forms nowadays."

"Quite, madam. Smithers, fetch Mrs. Medhurst, would you?"
Inspector Foster said.

Mrs. Ludlow turned her head stiffly to look at the Sergeant
as he obeyed. She called him back.

"You look a well set-up young man," she said, causing him
to blush furiously under his thatch of carroty hair. "You may
wheel me out."

Sergeant Smithers cast a glance at the Inspector, took the
handles of her chair, and turned her round. Mrs. Ludlow
directed him into the hall, and as they reached it Phyllis and
the gardener appeared from the kitchen and took charge.
Smithers was graciously dismissed by Mrs. Ludlow. He
returned to the study mopping his brow.

"Phew," he said. "Some character, that one, sir."

"Yes," agreed the Inspector. "Not many left like her these
days. Just as well, perhaps."

"I don't know. Total conformity is very dull," said the
Sergeant. He had enjoyed seeing his superior being routed.

"Hm. We'll give her time to get out into the garden, then
we'll take another look round upstairs," said the Inspector.
He frowned. "I should be very surprised if her relationship
with her family is as good as she implies," he said.

"She's not an easy individual at all," agreed the Sergeant,
meditating. "Mrs. Medhurst rather resembles her mother,
doesn't she, sir? Same tart manner. There's not much filial
love about in this house."

Inspector Foster glanced sharply at him. Really, Sergeant
Smithers was an odd young man; he used the most extraordinary phrases.

IV

When Patrick called at the home of his charge Tim Ludlow
on Monday afternoon, he saw as he approached the house the
figure of a sturdy, square woman wearing a shapeless skirt
standing in a large flower bed in the middle of the lawn. A
barrow filled with dead shoots was near her, and she was
struggling to uproot some tough plant that was defying all her
efforts. Patrick got out of the car and walked across the grass
towards her.

Betty saw him coming and stuck her fork in the ground.

She wiped her hands on her skirt and stepped out of the border on to the grass. She wore short wellington boots and patterned stockings that had caught on brambles and were laddered.

"I know, don't tell me, you're another policeman," she said, rubbing a hand over her forehead and leaving a grimy mark. "Two were here this morning."

"I'm not a policeman, Mrs. Ludlow," Patrick said. "I'm Patrick Grant, the Dean of St. Mark's."

"Oh God! What's happened now?" said Betty, and her face turned white. If he had not put out a hand to steady her, Patrick thought she might have stumbled. "It's Tim. Where is he?"

"Isn't he here?" asked Patrick. "I came to see him, as I'm staying in the neighbourhood."

"You mean he's all right? He hasn't got into trouble again?"

"As far as the university is concerned, I know of nothing wrong," Patrick said. "My visit is merely social. I apologise if I startled you. Of course, I've heard about the sad event in Winterswick. I've met your niece."

"You must think me very silly, Dr. Grant," said Betty, able to speak more calmly now that her immediate panic had been dispelled. "I felt sure Tim must be in trouble of some sort."

He is, thought Patrick, but his mother need not know about it yet. The apprehensive devotion which Betty Ludlow clearly felt for her worrying child was no new manifestation to Patrick.

"We've never met when you've been visiting Timothy at Mark's," he prompted her.

"No, we haven't. Oh, how rude of me, do come into the house, Dr. Grant," Betty said, recollecting herself.

"Well, if you're sure I won't be interrupting," Patrick said, with every intention of doing just that.

"Not at all. It will do me good to stop," said Betty. "I find gardening such a relaxation, don't you?"

This was a contradictory statement, and anything less relaxed than her own late occupation it would be hard to find, Patrick thought.

"I'm afraid I don't do much of it," he said. "But you must let me show you the Fellows' Garden when you come to Mark's next term; we have some very rare autumn-flowering shrubs."

"I'd like that," Betty said vaguely. She was not really listening.

She led the way into the house, apologising for taking him in by the back door, and paused in the lobby to shed her boots, exchanging them for a pair of shabby pumps.

"Would you like a cup of tea?" she offered.

Patrick thought she needed one herself, as shock treatment, and making it would help to soothe her, too. His plan of action for the next half-hour was one his sister would deplore. He grinned to himself, thinking of her reaction. Betty took him into the sitting-room and settled him down with the *Daily Mail* while she went to put the kettle on.

Left alone, Patrick at once got to his feet and inspected the room. It was large and comfortable, with shabby, well-worn chairs and a big, loose-cushioned sofa. There was no book in sight. Some knitting lay on a table, and there were photographs on the mantelpiece and on a large oak dresser by one wall. Patrick recognised Tim in adolescence, and more recently, before he grew his hair and adopted sideboards. There was another boy, too, a fairer, slimmer young man with a sensitive, anxious face; this one was like his mother. A second one of him, a wedding picture, showed him smiling with self-conscious pride beside his bride outside a church. Poor boy, no wonder he looked embarrassed; Patrick, well accustomed though he was to pageantry in Oxford, and to processing through the streets in his cap and doctor's robes of blue and scarlet, nevertheless considered any man who underwent the ordeal of the Church of England wedding ceremony in full regalia to be a hero. He was still looking at this photograph when Betty returned with a tea tray.

"Your other son?" he asked. "He's very like you."

"Oh, do you think so?" Betty was pleased. She put the tray on a low coffee table and they both sat down. "Yes, that's Martin. He's been married just over a year."

"What a very pretty girl," said Patrick.

"She's a model. She's kept her job on," Betty said, rather sadly, for unreasonably she had expected to become an instant grandmother. "They live in Chelsea. I'm sure she needn't work. Martin does quite well. He's with an advertising firm."

"Most young wives carry on with their jobs these days until they have a family," Patrick said. "It's sensible. They get bored otherwise."

"I suppose so," Betty said. She had become pregnant with

Martin on her honeymoon, and those early years after the war had been a nightmare of contriving, with food, soap and clothing, all rationed; it was a time when anxiety and over-work went hand-in-hand with motherhood, so different from today when parents could enjoy their babies.

"I expect you often see them?" Patrick asked.

"No, we don't," Betty said. "They're busy. They have their own friends. They don't come down to Sunday lunch at Pantons any more, I'm sorry to say. My mother-in-law has been very distressed about it. Old people mind these things."

"And Tim is away from home? I thought Cathy said he had come back from his holiday?" Patrick inquired.

"He got home on Saturday evening, but he went away again yesterday," Betty said. "I don't know where to," she added bleakly. How to explain the emotion that she felt, half fear for Tim, and half afraid of him, with his moods and his withdrawals? But there seemed to be no need; Dr. Grant appeared to be a very understanding man.

"They're secretive at that age," he said. "Wrapped up in themselves, and thoughtless. I shouldn't worry."

"No," said Betty doubtfully. It was vain advice; one could as well attempt to stop the tides.

"You said the police were here this morning?" Patrick felt that confidence had been established now and he could start to probe. "That's a sad business. Poor woman."

"Did you know that they think she may not have died a natural death?" said Betty, shuddering. Talking to Dr. Grant so frankly was not indiscreet; he seemed like an old friend. "It seems some of my mother-in-law's sleeping pills have disappeared. Yet I should never have thought Mrs. Macken-zie the suicidal type." She felt a sudden compulsion to con-fide in him. "The police are being very thorough. They want statements from us all about when we saw her last, and when we'd all been to Pantons."

Was this why Tim had disappeared, wondered Patrick, or was it for another reason?

"When did you last see her, Mrs. Ludlow?" he asked aloud.

"On Friday. My mother-in-law rang me up that afternoon while Mrs. Mackenzie was upstairs in her room and Phyllis was in Fennersham, and then my husband and I went round in the evening to welcome Gerald, that's my brother-in-law, and his wife back from their honeymoon. Oh, isn't it sad? We should all be happy now, for Gerald, instead of sad about Mrs. Mackenzie." And frightened. In an obscure way that she could not define Betty was frightened about Mrs. Mackenzie's death.

"It's very unfortunate," said Patrick. "She seemed quite well that night?" Better to go along with the suicide idea until the alternative was admitted.

"Oh yes," said Betty. "But then, people are deceptive."

Indeed they are, thought Patrick, even you, guileless though you seem. I wonder if the police noticed that you are terrified?

While Betty went on thinking that Patrick was a delightful, sympathetic man, he drew from her, bit by bit, an account of what had passed during her interview with Inspector Foster.

TUESDAY

I

The inquest was opened on Tuesday and adjourned for a week. Patrick sat at the back of the village school which was used for the proceedings, watching while Mrs. Mackenzie's son, Alec, a thin, pale young man with a stunned expression, gave evidence of identification. Phyllis Medhurst was present, soberly dressed in a grey suit and subdued feather hat, and both her brothers, but not their wives; afterwards the three conferred together in the school playground, watched interestedly over the wall by some of the pupils who were enjoying this unexpected day's holiday. Alec Mackenzie left the building with a young man whom Patrick recognised at once from his photograph as Martin Ludlow; after a few words with the older members of the family, the group broke up; Derek Ludlow patted his son on the shoulder and they all separated to their cars which were parked in the lane outside the school. Patrick got into his Rover and sat there lighting his pipe while Martin drove off in a dark Vauxhall Viva, with young Mackenzie as his passenger.

"Curiouser and curiouser," said Patrick to himself as he drove slowly back to Reynard's.

The fine weather had broken and a gentle rain was falling. After lunch Jane and Andrew had a date at the clinic; she might be away some time, Jane said, as she might go back for a cup of tea with one of the other mothers. Patrick settled down for an afternoon's work with his papers. It was intriguing to speculate on what had motivated people's actions centuries ago: much the same things as drove on their successors now, he thought, greed, envy, lust. He soon found his mind

71

wandering away from Chipping Campden towards Pantons and the mystery there.

At three o'clock the front door bell rang, and when Patrick answered it he found standing on the step Inspector Foster, whom he had seen at the inquest earlier, and his red-haired Sergeant.

"Dr. Patrick Grant?" inquired the Inspector.

"Yes," Patrick said. "What can I do for you, Inspector? Will you come in?"

He led the way into Jane's sitting-room, and removed a rattle and a small woolly duck from a chair so that the Inspector could sit down. "My nephew's," he explained, and sat down opposite after finding another chair for the Sergeant.

"This will be your sister's house, I believe? Mrs. Conway?" asked the Inspector.

"That is correct," said Patrick.

"I'm making some inquiries into the death of Mrs. Joyce Mackenzie," said the Inspector. "There are one or two points you may be able to help me with."

"I am at your service, Inspector," Patrick said.

"You were at the inquest, were you not?" the Inspector asked.

"I was. A sad business."

"Yes. A shock for the lady's son, I'm afraid. He's taken it hard."

"A shock for everyone," Patrick suggested. "But perhaps in your job you become inured to these things?"

"To some extent," said the Inspector guardedly. "It depends upon the circumstances. When it's a youngster—never." He cleared his throat and rattled his papers. "Well now, sir," he said. "I believe you went up to the Stable House on Saturday evening. Will you tell me how that came about, please?"

"Certainly, Inspector. I went to Pantons, too, and met the deceased lady," Patrick said. He watched to see if this was news to the Inspector.

"Did you? Please tell me what occurred," said the Inspector with a poker face.

"I was collecting for charity," Patrick explained. "I went up on behalf of my sister, who had been round the rest of the village. I had met Miss Cathy Ludlow, whose cousin, Timothy Ludlow, is a member of my college. I went to Pantons first, and the door was opened by a woman who must have been the late Mrs. Mackenzie. Plump, grey-haired, about fifty. She had very blue eyes and wore a green overall."

Silently the Inspector handed him a photograph, and Patrick nodded.

"Yes," he said.

"What time was this?" asked the Inspector.

"About twenty-five past eight, I should say."

"Did you see anyone else?"

"No. Mrs. Mackenzie disappeared briefly and came back with five shillings, which she gave me, and I left."

"You waited on the step meanwhile?"

"She invited me into the hall."

"Did she go upstairs to get the money from her employer, do you think?"

"She did not go up the front staircase. I imagine there is another in a house of that size. But she was not very long."

"Hm." The Inspector made a note in his book. "Did you happen to notice that there was an oak chest in the hall?" he asked.

"Yes," said Patrick, who had stood there noticing everything from the prints on the walls to the state of the barometer during the housekeeper's absence.

"There were a number of objects on it. Can you recall what any of them were?"

Patrick had always been good at Kim's game.

"There were some car keys, a pile of books—novels from the library, I should imagine," he said, knowing very well what they were and all their titles. "Some gloves, a torch, the parish magazine, and a small parcel."

"You're very observant, Dr. Grant."

"I try to be," said Patrick modestly.

"What size was the parcel?"

"Oh, very small. A little paper bag, about two inches square, or less."

The Inspector took from his pocket a small paper bag printed with the name of the chemist, Fennersham.

"Like this?"

"It could have been. That size, anyway," Patrick agreed. He sighed. "The fatal pills, eh? Of course I didn't know then what was in the parcel, so I can't tell you whether the bottle was half-empty at the time I called, or whether they vanished later. What a pity."

Jane, of course, had so low an opinion of him that she

would have expected him to pry during his brief spell of solitude.

"You seem well-informed about the manner in which Mrs. Mackenzie died," said the Inspector disapprovingly.

"My sister and Cathy Ludlow are friends," Patrick said. "Cathy was very distressed by this whole business, naturally enough, and she told us what had happened."

"I see. I hope I can rely on your discretion, Dr. Grant?" said the Inspector. "I am anxious to keep this quiet at present. I don't want the Press down here."

"I share your anxiety," Patrick said. "My sister and I only want to help our friends."

"After Mrs. Mackenzie had given you a donation, you went to the Stable House?"

"I did. I must have reached there soon after half-past eight."

"And who was present?"

"Mr. and Mrs. Gerald Ludlow, Mrs. Medhurst, and Cathy Ludlow," Patrick said. "They kindly invited me in and gave me a drink as well as some contributions."

"And you remained there for how long?"

"Oh, about three-quarters of an hour. Perhaps a little longer," Patrick said. "We had a pleasant time."

"And everyone you have named was present all the while?"

"Yes. That is—" Patrick hesitated, but someone else, Cathy for instance, would tell the Inspector if he did not. "Mrs. Ludlow left the room briefly to fetch her purse, which was upstairs. She put ten shillings in the tin."

"And Mr. Ludlow contributed as well?"

"Yes. He gave me a pound," said Patrick.

"Did you not think it surprising for Mrs. Ludlow to contribute on her own account?"

"I thought it generous," said Patrick. "I knew that she had not been married long and perhaps did not realise it wasn't necessary. Her husband made some such comment, as a matter of fact."

"She was gone only briefly? Just long enough to fetch the money from her bedroom?"

"Well, no, Inspector. She was a little longer than that," said Patrick. "She probably took time to powder her nose and so forth. You know what women are."

"Dr. Grant, in your opinion, would there have been time for her to have gone up to Pantons and returned again?"

"You're not suggesting, are you Inspector, that Mrs. Gerald Ludlow sprinted up to the big house to put sleeping pills in the fruit pie in order to murder the mother-in-law she'd only just met? Anyway, all but the fatal slice had been eaten by this time."

"I'm not suggesting anything, Dr. Grant," said Inspector Foster coldly. "I'm asking you a question."

"I didn't time the lady," Patrick said smoothly. He glanced towards the Sergeant, busy with his shorthand, ginger eyebrows twitching.

"So the pills *were* in the pie?" Patrick said.

Inspector Foster looked at him, meditating. Then he said: "I'll tell you this in confidence, sir. We've had the analyst's report, and a quantity of barbiturate was found in the deceased's stomach, together with partially digested lemon meringue pie and enough whisky to suggest that she had consumed two or more doubles before retiring."

"I see," said Patrick. "I appreciate your confidence, Inspector."

"The powder could have been in the whisky, but it doesn't dissolve readily, and there was no trace of any such adulteration in the glass in the dead woman's room or in the bottle she kept in her cupboard."

"So it all points the other way," Patrick said slowly. "If only I'd looked inside the chemist's parcel when I was in the hall. If Mrs. Mackenzie was bent on suicide she might not have taken the pills out of the bottle until later, when she went to bed." He looked at the Inspector. "We have suicides in Oxford you know," he said. "Youngsters who can't cope. It's easy to be wise afterwards, of course, but Mrs. Mackenzie didn't look disturbed in any way."

"No, sir."

"So you've got a case of murder here," said Patrick. "What a dreadful thing."

"I'm not agreeing with you, sir," said the Inspector grimly. "I'm just investigating every possibility, at present."

Patrick nodded.

"Quite so," he said.

"Would you tell me what time you left the Stable House, Dr. Grant?" the Inspector asked.

"About a quarter past nine," said Patrick.

"You had your car?"

"No, I walked. I wanted the exercise."

The Inspector would ask if he had seen anyone as he

returned to Reynard's, and he would have to say that Martin Ludlow's Vauxhall Viva had passed him in the drive. Only citizens totally lacking in a sense of responsibility withheld information likely to assist the police. Patrick waited for the question, but to his surprise it did not come.

"Thank you, Dr. Grant. You've been most helpful," the Inspector said, rising to go. "If you think of anything else, I'm sure you'll get in touch with me. Apart from old Mrs. Ludlow, you were the last person to see Mrs. Mackenzie alive."

"I will of course," Patrick assured him, earnestly. In his pocket was the envelope addressed to young Tim Ludlow which he had found that night, and in his pocket it would stay until that youth had explained his movements. For the present, the Inspector must dree his own weird, and a pretty confused one it appeared to be.

Jane came back from her afternoon's expedition in time to see the police car drive away from the cottage.

"What's been going on?" she demanded, hurrying into the house with the baby in her arms.

"Inspector Foster wanted my assistance," Patrick said, with a complacent air.

"Don't give me that. It's a pity he couldn't arrest you and lock you up out of the way," Jane said.

Patrick ignored this gibe.

"My collection of the facts is being hampered because I have yet to meet the formidable Mrs. Ludlow," he said. "I think I'll rectify the matter. If I go up to Pantons this evening, I'll catch her before she goes to bed."

"You can't go bursting in up there when they're in all this trouble," said Jane.

"Yes, I can. I can carry our condolences and offer them our help," said Patrick. "And I'd quite like to see how little Cathy's getting on."

"Now lay off her. She's just at the age to fall for an older man," Jane warned. "Don't add cradle-snatching or infant heart-break to your list of sins."

"It won't hurt her at all to have a little crush on me," said Patrick smugly. "Form her taste for her. Quite beneficial, I should say."

"Oh you!" cried Jane, exasperated. "Andrew, here's a most conceited man. Don't you grow up like him, my precious poppet," and she bore her baby away, out of the contaminating presence of his uncle.

II

It was Cathy who opened the door when he rang the bell at Pantons some time later. Her face brightened when she saw him.

"Hullo, Cathy. How's everything? I just came to see if you're all bearing up, and if there's anything I can do," he said.

"Come in," Cathy said. She looked round, and added in a whisper, "it's awful. It's agony waiting for something more to happen."

"Who is it? Who's out there?" called a deep voice from the drawing-room.

Cathy made a face.

"That's Gran. We'll have to go in," she muttered, and led the way.

"It's Dr. Grant, Grandmother," she said, as he followed her into the room.

"How do you do, Mrs. Ludlow," Patrick said, walking towards the corner by the fireplace where the old lady sat. "My sister and I are so very sorry to hear about what has happened. I came to see if I could be of any assistance to you at this time."

"How good of you, Dr. Grant," said Mrs. Ludlow. She surveyed him imperially from top to toe in her frank manner, as he stood there calmly, staring back at her. She was a dominating presence, even in her chair. He saw the neat, proud head, defiantly held in spite of age, the piercing eyes, the hands clasped on her lap above a silver-headed stick laid across her knees. She looked very small, but it was difficult to tell if this were a true impression or one caused by her crippling illness.

"Come along and sit down, Dr. Grant," she said at last, pointing to a chair that faced her. "Cathy, pour Dr. Grant some sherry."

Cathy obeyed, and then sat down on the window seat, riveting her gaze on Patrick in a fashion that he found flattering, but mildly disconcerting in view of Jane's recent remarks.

"This is a sad business," he said.

"It's most unfortunate," said Mrs. Ludlow. "She was a good cook."

Patrick was at once reminded of Lady Macbeth.

"I can't see why the police need to make so much of it," the old lady went on. "She must have had a heart attack. But I understand there are formalities."

Obviously Mrs. Ludlow could not be told that the police suspected a member of her family had set out to poison her, and the wrong person had taken the poison. Playing for time was clearly the line being taken; she could doubtless be strung along for some days by this means, and her immobility would prevent her from stumbling on the truth. But she would have to know in the end.

"You have a lovely house, Mrs. Ludlow," Patrick said, changing the tack, and felt Cathy breathe a sigh of relaxation.

"I'm glad you admire it, Dr. Grant. It was built for me when I came here as a bride," Mrs. Ludlow said. "All my children were born here, and so was Cathy. You doubtless know that my husband gave his life for his country in the First World War?"

"Yes. I'm sorry," Patrick murmured. The archaic phrase was oddly moving; he perceived that she had never recovered from this blow.

"He was a good man, a real man," she said. "There is his photograph." She pointed to one in a silver frame that stood on the table beside her.

Patrick dutifully rose and inspected the photograph, which showed a young man in captain's uniform. He had a neat moustache and a steady expression, but these did not mask the sensitivity of the face that was repeated in Cathy's.

"A fine-looking man," said Patrick, feeling this to be a most inadequate comment. He wondered if the owner of those fine-drawn features had really been as tough as his widow seemed to believe.

"Yes," said Mrs. Ludlow. "And he would have been disappointed in the young of today if he had lived to see them."

Patrick doubted it; the mouth in the photograph was generous and mobile; the eyes had a faraway look; it was neither a saint's nor an ascetic's face, but nor was it that of a bigot.

"Gran finds everyone a disappointment after Grandfather," Cathy observed. "Even her own children."

"Not your father," Mrs. Ludlow said. "He's the only one to come anywhere near your grandfather." She turned to Patrick. "Cathy's father was born after my husband died. I named him Gerald, for his father." She went silent after this, brooding to herself, and rocked a little as she sat. Cathy exchanged an alarmed glance with Patrick.

"Gran, are you all right? Do you want one of your little red pills?" she asked.

"Of course not. Don't be ridiculous, girl," snapped the old lady. "Red pills, white pills, blue pills. It's all pills these days," she grumbled. "And other pills too, for girls who should know better. What a world! I suppose you get a lot of that at Oxford, Dr. Grant?"

"Girls who should know better, do you mean? Oh, and young men too," said Patrick. "After all, it takes two to make that sort of mistake, doesn't it?"

Cathy snorted at this and had to pretend to cough. To her astonishment a wintry smile appeared among the lines on her grandmother's face.

"Cathy has some foolish notion of going to Oxford," Mrs. Ludlow said. "I tell her she'd be wasting her time and her father's money, of which he's little enough as it is."

"Father can afford it, Gran. He wants me to go," said Cathy.

"Why don't you approve, Mrs. Ludlow?" asked Patrick. "I should have thought you'd be an ardent feminist." He could easily imagine her campaigning for the vote. But then he realised that all her latent energy had turned inwards, towards her family.

"A woman needs a man to look after and a nursery of children. That's her function," Mrs. Ludlow said. "One your aunt Phyllis has signally failed to fulfil, Cathy. Don't follow her example."

Here it was; this was the bitter intolerance that Patrick had been told about. But Cathy was not going to let it pass. She went bright red but spoke up boldly.

"Gran, that isn't fair," she said. "Aunt Phyl's had rotten luck. You shouldn't talk like that about her. And where would I be now, but for her?" She didn't quite dare to add, "or you, come to that."

Good for Cathy, Patrick thought. He sent her an approving glance.

"She married a little pipsqueak, so what did she expect? Marry a proper man, Cathy, and then you won't go wrong," said Mrs. Ludlow. "Someone like Dr. Grant here. You're married, of course?" she asked, turning to him fiercely.

"I'm not, as a matter of fact," Patrick admitted.

At this moment, fortunately perhaps, Phyllis Medhurst came into the room.

"Ah, Dr. Grant, I wondered who was here. What a nice surprise," she said, with her pleasant smile.

Patrick rose to greet her, and wondered how her mother failed to see the likeable woman so clearly recognised by everybody else.

"Dr. Grant kindly called to offer sympathy," said Mrs. Ludlow. "He's in charge of Tim, I think you said, Phyllis?"

Phyllis agreed.

"Hm. A very spoilt young man," pronounced his grandmother. "His mother and his aunt here have made a fool of him by letting him do exactly as he wanted all his life. Now he's a wastrel."

"Oh, hardly that," protested Patrick. "A lot of young men go through a phase which can be very trying for the older people who have to deal with them."

"I would not permit my children to behave as the young of today do," said Mrs. Ludlow.

"You're too harsh, Mother," Phyllis said.

"You know nothing about it, Phyllis. You have no children of your own," said Mrs. Ludlow.

Phyllis turned that ugly, dull red that Patrick had seen before. She got to her feet without a word and walked towards the door, but Mrs. Ludlow called her back.

"Phyllis, I will stay up for dinner tonight," she said. "I'm hoping Dr. Grant will join us. Will you?" she asked, and gazed upon him genially.

Patrick demurred, but only slightly; he was eager to stay, and when Phyllis and Cathy both urged him to accept the invitation, he agreed, and telephoned to Jane who had plenty to say to him about his sordid motives. But he saw that Phyllis and Cathy could be helped if he acted as a buffer between them and the old lady, so throughout the meal he set out to charm her. He could talk entertainingly on a number of subjects, and despite his remark to Betty Ludlow he knew a good deal about certain aspects of horticulture, so that he was able to discuss intelligently what plants were hard to grow in this area and to marvel appropriately when Mrs.

Ludlow claimed success with them. She promised to show the garden to him when he called again.

After the meal she allowed Phyllis to wheel her towards the lift at the back of the hall, up to bed, and Patrick helped Cathy clear away.

"Gran took a fancy to you," Cathy said. Watching her grandmother's response to him had been a revelation.

"She's remarkable," he said with truth. "So's your aunt."

"Aunt Phyl's a darling," Cathy said, and added, "Gran's so mean to her."

"It's odd, that," Patrick said. "Perhaps they're too much alike to get on well together."

Cathy stared.

"I don't think Aunt Phyl's a bit like Gran," she said. "She's much kinder."

Patrick did not think it would be prudent to say that he could imagine Phyllis growing into quite a formidable person if she had power to wield.

"What happened to the charlotte russe?" he asked, as they stacked the plates in the dishwasher.

"Fancy you remembering it! None of us could bear to touch it," Cathy said. "We threw it away." She hesitated. "You were at the inquest, weren't you? Father said so."

"Yes, I was."

"You saw Alec Mackenzie. Martin brought him up here. He was absolutely stunned. He couldn't believe his mother would ever commit suicide. I've been thinking."

"Yes? What have you thought, Cathy?"

"About that pie. The lemon meringue, I mean. It was meant for Gran, wasn't it? By chance she didn't eat it, and poor Mrs. Mack did." She looked up at Patrick with enormous, solemn eyes. "It was one of us, wasn't it, one of the family I mean, who did it?" As she said the words the full implication of them swept over her.

Patrick spoke impulsively.

"Cathy, come down and stay with us till this is over. You're too young to be mixed up with it," he said.

She drew herself up and looked at him again, this time with a proud expression; he saw the family resemblance, and he saw his error.

"I'm not a child," she said. "I have to stay." Then her face softened, and she added, "But thank you, all the same."

"I'm sorry. You're right. You must stay. Forget it," Patrick said. "I just wanted to get you out of the horrors."

"What frightens me is that whoever it was might try again," Cathy confessed.

"I don't think you need be afraid of that," said Patrick. "Whoever it was will have had a bad fright and won't risk another attempt."

"Are you sure?"

"Yes," said Patrick firmly.

"The police are bound to find out who it was?"

"I expect so," Patrick said. "In time."

"But one of us! Aunt Phyl, or Father, or Uncle Derek! It can't be true! She's awful, I know, and very cruel, but to want her dead! I can't believe it's true," said Cathy, and Jane would have looked very ironically on the scene that followed as Cathy wept bitterly and Patrick mopped her up.

To help her, he decided to invent.

"It could have been an outsider, someone from the past," he said. "You were all out on Saturday night. Someone may have called. Only Mrs. Mackenzie would have known if that was so." As it was, at least three people had been there that night, himself and the two Ludlow boys.

"Oh, could that have happened?" At this new idea Cathy looked more cheerful.

"It's possible. Your grandmother has lived a long time and she may have made some enemies. It might be someone with a grudge going back for years."

"Oh, it might, mightn't it?" Cathy clutched at this. "Gran is a great one for feuds. She wouldn't talk to Mrs. Bligh for twenty years, because the 'Blighs cut their spinney down and when it was burnt the smoke all blew this way."

"There you are, then. There must have been other things like that. One of your grandmother's old enemies has become a nut and sought revenge," said Patrick.

"If they saw the tray, they'd know it was for Gran," Cathy said. "But how would they find the pills, or get past Mrs. Mack?"

"They might have hidden somewhere. In the lift, perhaps, waiting for their chance," Patrick invented wildly. She was much too sharp. She'd see through it very soon. It was a red herring and he doubted if it would last her for the night, but it might.

When Phyllis came downstairs they were sitting peaceably together in the drawing-room drinking their coffee, and Patrick had his diary out, planning a date for her to come to lunch next term and be taken round to meet his aunt, the Principal of St. Joan's.

III

"And then?" demanded Jane. She was waiting on the sofa reading when Patrick arrived back at Reynard's, with a Rachmaninov record playing, waiting to hear how he had employed the evening.

"Gerald and Helen Ludlow came up after dinner. He seems a decent sort of chap; hidden fires, I'd say—not much visible on the surface but plenty there in fact. She's rather reserved."

"You'd be reserved if you'd just got married and found yourself in the midst of a murder," said Jane. "What's her history? Cathy doesn't seem to know much about her."

"So you've been giving way to vulgar curiosity too, have you?" Patrick teased her.

"We had this conversation some time ago, when Cathy first heard about the marriage," Jane said primly. "It didn't matter then. We weren't mixed up with melodrama."

"She was a widow," Patrick said. "You knew that. Presumably an impecunious one, since she was companion to some wealthy American woman. But there may have been a particular reason for her to want that sort of job; she may have had a yen for travel or something. I can't see her as a go-getting career girl *per se*, but she might be a scholarly type. Her relationship with her husband intrigues me; he's badly smitten, there's no doubt of that, but it's less easy to observe her feelings."

"If she's reserved, as you say, she probably saves her demonstrations for when they're alone, and quite right too," said Jane austerely.

"She may have married for security," Patrick said. "It's been known." He mused. "She's not a girl—I'd say she's about thirty-four."

"Do you find her attractive?" Jane inquired with interest.

She had often wondered what sort of woman appealed to her brother.

"I'm not sure," Patrick said. "She'd be a challenge—she seems so well controlled. She has potential, shall we say?"

"Hm. Well, who's your favourite candidate for the role of murderer?" Jane asked.

"I'm still guessing," Patrick said. "I have an idea, but it needs some facts to back it. I'm still in the dark about the motivation behind all this, and I haven't yet met Derek Ludlow. I saw him at the inquest, but I haven't spoken to him."

"You should tell the police that those two grandsons were at Pantons on Saturday night," Jane said. "It's their job to decide what's relevant, not yours."

"The boys must have a chance to account for themselves first," said Patrick. "No one seems to know where Tim is, but Martin's address is no secret. I shall go and call on him tomorrow."

"What do you hope to find out from him?"

"The truth about his marital problems. His mother seems to think things are dicey there. He may have money worries, or problems connected with his work. The most obvious thing is that he wanted to touch his grandmother for a loan. I gather from Cathy that she holds the purse-strings pretty tightly. She's a rich woman, but she controls everything herself. Cathy's father has done very well in business, but without any help from his mother."

"So I should hope," said Jane.

"Yes. But Derek has been through some rough times. It might have been reasonable to expect a little rescue operation, when the children were young and he was finding it hard to get going after the war. However, nothing doing. And Cathy doesn't think Phyllis has much cash. Of course, she doesn't need a lot, living free."

"Free, but not independent," Jane said. "Cathy seems to have waxed very confidential."

"She did," Patrick said happily.

Jane gave him a look.

"I wish you wouldn't interfere," she said. "It's your duty to tell the police all you know, instead of poking about quizzily on the edge of this affair."

"Ah, but it's so interesting," Patrick said. "And I'm managing to work my way into the middle of it. I'm really helping the cause of justice by finding out things they'd never think about."

"The police would get there in the end," said Jane. "How do you suppose they manage when you aren't around? And they've got all the equipment—fingerprint kit and so on. You're only equipped with curiosity."

"You forget my trained mind," Patrick said. "This case is a question of character. Personalities are what matter. Is it a crime of passion, or of greed?"

"Hardly passion, surely, with a woman of nearly eighty in the centre of the web?"

"I'm not so sure. There is passion here. Gerald's for his wife, Betty's for her son, perhaps even Phyllis is affected by passion of a kind," said Patrick. "We shall have to wait and see."

WEDNESDAY

I

Phyllis Medhurst walked along Fennersham High Street carrying a loaded shopping basket and two library books. She entered the Cobweb Café, looked about her for a moment, and then went quickly towards a corner table where a large man with a bald head and spectacles was already seated.

"Phyllis, my dear," he said, rising to greet her. He took her packages and stowed them out of the way, and held her chair for her. Then he signalled to the waitress and ordered coffee for them both.

"Well, how are you?" he asked.

Phyllis looked at him.

"I can never lie to you, Maurice," she said. "You see through me straight away. I'm desperate."

"My dear, why not let me help you?"

"You can't, Maurice. You must keep out of the way till this is all over. Then we'll think of something," she said.

"But it's ridiculous to go on like this," said Maurice. "Snatching chances to meet, like a pair of children whose parents aren't on speaking terms."

"If you come to church in Winterswick again there'll soon be talk," said Phyllis, but she smiled.

"Ah, that's better," Maurice said. He pressed her hand for an instant. "What's wrong, my dear? Aren't the police satisfied?"

Phyllis shook her head.

"Phyllis, I'm completely in the dark. I only have the very confused account of what has happened that you gave me on the telephone."

"I'm sorry, Maurice. It's too risky to say more," said Phyllis. She sighed. "I expect the *Fennersham Gazette* will have something about it on Friday. But the less you know the better." She looked anxiously around her as she spoke. "Besides, someone might hear us."

"Well, come back to the bungalow, where we can't be overheard," he said.

"I can't, I must get home. My new sister-in-law and my niece are looking after Mother, and she'll play them up."

"You can't go on like this, my dear," said Maurice. He looked at her in a concerned way. "I'll come up and see you this afternoon."

"No, don't!" she exclaimed. "How could I explain about you?"

"You could say I am a friend," he said mildly. "Surely you can have your friends to visit you?"

How could she tell him that she no longer invited anyone to Pantons, because her mother was either offensive to her in front of them, or mocked at them when they had gone? One by one she had lost the few friends of her youth so that apart from her visits to the library and her weekly art classes—a recent venture—she had no outside contacts until now.

"You'll think me very stupid," she said. "But Mother wants to know everything that happens to any of us. If you came to the house she'd be dreadfully curious and rude. It wouldn't be worth while. In fact it might be easiest if we never met again," she added wildly. "I don't want to involve you in my problems."

"You don't mean that," Maurice told her gravely. "Friendship means helping out with troubles."

"Oh, I know, but it's all so difficult," said Phyllis. How could he understand that if her mother knew she occasionally had tea in Fennersham with a retired, widowed bank manager, sometimes went for walks with him in the park or had a glass of sherry at his bungalow, and met him for coffee every Wednesday morning when she did the shopping, she would be taunted in the crudest way?

"You can't go on under this strain, my dear," he now said firmly. "You'll have to shed some of it."

"I'll sort it out when this business about Mrs. Mackenzie is all over," Phyllis said. "I can't start looking for another housekeeper till then. Who would want to come, knowing what has happened?"

"I wish you'd tell me what it is," said Maurice. "You make it sound so mysterious."

"It is mysterious," Phyllis said. She lowered her voice. "Some of mother's pills have vanished. No one knows quite whether Mrs. Mackenzie meant to kill herself, or if it was even worse than that. I can't say any more. Don't ask me to."

He stared at her, appalled. Then he accepted what she said.

"Promise to ring me up at any hour, day or night, if I can help you," he said.

She nodded. It was easy to agree.

"We'll talk about something else now," she said, and asked about his married daughter.

When they had finished their coffee he carried her shopping to the car, which was parked near the market square. Then he watched her drive away, back to shoulder all her burdens.

And someone else watched both of them, a nondescript man in a shabby raincoat, who followed Maurice home and then walked quickly off towards the nearest telephone kiosk.

II

"But Tim, what are you going to do about it?" Cathy asked.

They were sitting on the low wall that divided the rose garden from the long lawn; this was a place where they could safely talk without being overheard, for they could see if anyone approached. It had been raining earlier, and the air still held a misty dampness that was typical of autumn.

"You'll have to get the money," Cathy went on. "I've got twelve pounds in the post office; you can borrow that, and perhaps we could pawn our christening presents or something, silver's pretty valuable just now."

"Thanks, Cath, but twelve pounds would be only a drop in the ocean," said Tim gloomily. He swung his legs to and fro, kicking the moss-covered wall with his rubber heels. "I've got to get hold of two hundred and fifty."

"Couldn't you pay in instalments?" Cathy said. She sniffed. "Tim, don't you ever have a bath? You positively stink. What's come over you? You never used to be like this." She looked distastefully at her cousin. His hair reached well below his ears, and hung in greasy rats' tails; he wore a grubby sweater and torn jeans, and canvas shoes through one of which a dirty toe protruded.

"Lay off me, Cathy, can't you? I've been travelling all night. You can't keep clean when you're hitching lifts in lorries," Tim said sulkily.

"It's not only what you look like. You've got so messy altogether. Fancy getting into a scrape like this," said Cathy. "It's all so unnecessary. Can't you pull yourself together? We've got enough worry to face without you behaving like a delinquent."

"Oh hark at our virtuous prefect," Tim said in a jeering voice. "You've left school now. Grow up, Cathy. There are worse problems in the world than those in your St. Trinian's code."

"Yes, there are," said Cathy hotly. "And Mrs. Mackenzie's murder is one of them."

As soon as the words were said she put her hand across her mouth, but it was too late.

"Murder! Did you say *murder*?" Tim gasped.

She nodded.

"You'd have to know eventually," she said. "If you hadn't gone rushing off like a lunatic you'd have known all about it."

"But she had a heart attack."

"She didn't. She had some of Gran's sleeping pills. Quite a lot of them, in fact. And they were really meant for Gran," Cathy said. "There. Perhaps that'll shake you, Timothy Ludlow. Maybe you'll get your priorities a bit sorted out now."

"But I don't understand," Tim said. "How could it be like that?"

He listened meekly while Cathy explained what had happened: how Grandmother had not eaten her pudding and how the powder from the capsules could have been mixed into the meringue.

"Dr. Grant says it's got a very bitter taste, but lemon meringue has contrasting flavours anyway. You might scarcely realise until you'd swallowed it," she said.

"But who would want to do Gran in?"

Cathy shrugged.

"Dr. Grant thinks it may be someone from the past, with a grudge," she said. "But I don't. I don't see how an outsider would have known she'd be alone with Mrs. Mack that night, or where to find the pudding. I think it must be one of the family. Isn't it awful, Tim?"

"My God, it is," he said. Under its grime, his face turned pale. "Cathy, are you sure you couldn't find that letter?" he said, and seized her wrist.

She pulled free.

"Keep your mitts off me," she said. "I've told you already, I looked everywhere for it after you asked me about it on Sunday, including hunting through three dustbins, and it isn't here. You must have lost it somewhere else."

"But I must have dropped it here," Tim said. "I came up on Saturday to ask Aunt Phyl if she'd lend me the money. I knew she would if she'd got it. She let me have a cheque for thirty pounds, that's all she could manage. She hasn't any money of her own. Did you know that? Not a bean, and Gran doesn't give her any for herself."

Cathy stared.

"I know Gran pays all the bills and things," she said. "But how does Aunt Phyl buy clothes, and the presents she gives us?"

"Your father makes her an allowance. It's because she's always looked after you," Tim told her. "You didn't know about it?"

Cathy shook her head.

"Poor Aunt Phyl. She could have had a job and earned a proper salary. She does more for Gran than three paid people would," said Cathy.

"I think Uncle Gerald gives her quite a bit, really, but not so that she could suddenly produce over two hundred pounds," said Tim. "She said she could give me some more next month, but it will be too late then. None of my friends can help. That's where I've been, seeing if anyone could."

"Well, you must tell your parents. They'll lend you the rest," said Cathy.

"I can't. I tried. Dad thought I just wanted my allowance early, but he said things have gone wrong at the office and he may not be able to let me have anything at all. Not even my allowance for next term."

"Oh, no!"

"It's true. Mother stumped up twenty, but that was her limit," Tim said. "I didn't tell them why I wanted it. Dad didn't give me a chance, actually. He seems to be in rather a fix. I may not be able to go back to Mark's."

"Oh Tim! What can have happened?"

Tim shrugged.

"I don't know," he said. "Cathy, do you think the police found that letter? They were here on Sunday, weren't they? Before I asked you to look?"

"They may have. If so, you'll be hearing from them," Cathy said.

"Oh, you don't care," Tim said bitterly.

"Since you mention it, I don't. I think you're a silly idiot and you deserve a lesson, but your mother doesn't and neither does poor Uncle Derek, especially if he's in some other trouble."

"But don't you see, if the police found that letter, they'll guess I was here on Saturday, and they'll know I wanted money. They may suspect me of wanting to murder Gran," Tim said. "We all know we'll get something when she dies, and Gran is loaded."

"Our parents will get it."

"There's some in trust for us. You must know that."

"I never think about it," Cathy said. "It's vile, waiting for dead men's shoes." She turned and gave him a sharp look. "Did you see Gran that night?" she asked.

He did not answer.

"Tim, did you?"

"I decided to try her when I drew blank with Aunt Phyl," he admitted at last.

"She wouldn't help you," Cathy stated.

"No. She gave me a fearful rocket," Tim said.

"Good for her," said Cathy. "But when was all this? I never heard you."

"You were having a bath," Tim said.

"Aunt Phyl never told me you'd been to the house."

"She wouldn't. She's a brick," Tim said. "And the chances are she won't have told the police either. But they'll know, if they found that letter."

"Oh, you make me sick," stormed Cathy. "Can't you think of anyone but yourself? Mrs. Mack is dead. She had everything to live for, children who loved her, and grandchildren too. She was knitting a cardigan for one of the little girls. And we were fond of her, as well. And she's dead, because someone, one of the family, wanted to kill Gran."

"But the police may think it was me," Tim said.

"Well, you'll just have to talk them out of it, won't you?" Cathy said. She sprang off the wall and ran away from him across the garden, her feet in sandals squeaking on the damp grass and her hair streaming out behind her as she went.

Tim got off the wall too. Head down, hands in his pockets, he slouched away over the lawn towards the drive.

III

Martin Ludlow awoke with a splitting headache and a sour taste in his mouth. He lay very still in bed, listening to the throbbing in his head, while the events of the past days, culminating with the previous evening, came back to him. He thought about Sandra, and reached across the bed to see if she had changed her mind, as had happened once before, but he was alone. It was over, then.

After a while, groaning, he got out of bed and tottered into the bathroom. He had managed to get as far as the kitchen, and was sitting in front of a cup of inky coffee and four aspirins, when the door-bell rang.

On the doorstep stood a tall, well-built man with heavy-rimmed spectacles. He looked vaguely familiar, even when seen through half-closed, peering, bloodshot eyes.

"Good morning, Mr. Ludlow," said Patrick briskly. "I am Patrick Grant, Dean of St. Mark's. Can you spare me a few minutes? I'm glad to have caught you before you leave for your office."

His vigorous tones struck at Martin's pounding head like hammer blows.

"What's that young idiot Tim done now?" he mumbled. "Come in, won't you? I'm afraid you've caught me at a bad moment."

This was obvious. Apart from his own condition, the place was in a chaotic state, with empty bottles, loaded ashtrays, and dirty glasses everywhere, and the air was stale with tobacco fumes.

"There was a party. I'm a bit hung-over," Martin confessed.

"You do look a bit green," Patrick said, regarding him with some sympathy and an experienced eye.

"I was just going to swig down some coffee and some aspirins," Martin said. "Can I offer you a cup?"

"Thank you," Patrick said. "But let me get it." He looked at the younger man consideringly. "I suppose you haven't any

Fernet Branca?" he asked, and when Martin shook his head, said, "Pity. It's good for your condition. Never mind. There are other remedies. How about letting me mix something for you, if you've got the ingredients? A little of the hair of the dog, plus a few things from the kitchen cupboard. May I look? My scout's a dab hand at a prairie oyster."

"Help yourself," said Martin, sinking down into a chair.

Patrick bustled about, finding eggs, brandy and worcester sauce readily to hand. He spared a thought for his room at Mark's, where cartons of tiny Underberg bottles were always in stock for these emergencies. Still, what was here would do. He stirred the mixture and gave it to the patient.

Presently, Martin began to look a little better.

"I'm awfully sorry," he said. "I'm not often in this state."

"Don't worry. It happens to us all," said Patrick. "In any case this is an unreasonable hour to call, but I don't know where you work and I didn't want to ask your mother. This has nothing to do with Timothy, or only indirectly. It's about the late Mrs. Mackenzie."

"Oh, that's where I saw you! At the inquest yesterday. I've been trying to remember," Martin said.

"I was there," Patrick said. "Have the police been to see you yet?"

"No. Why should they?"

"You were at Pantons on Saturday night," Patrick said. "I was in the drive when you left, at about nine-fifteen."

There was a silence.

"Oh," said Martin, at last.

"It is 'oh,' isn't it?" Patrick said. "Why were you there?"

Martin groaned and clasped his head.

"Do the police know?" he asked.

"I'm sure they do," said Patrick untruthfully. "What will you tell them? They're certain to inquire."

"The truth, I suppose," said Martin. "That I wanted to borrow some money from my grandmother."

"Did she lend you what you wanted?"

"Not she. Read me a lecture instead," said Martin ruefully. "It doesn't matter now, anyway. Sandra's gone. I don't suppose it would have stopped her."

"Hm." Patrick looked consideringly at the young man. "You know where Alec Mackenzie lives, don't you? You brought him down yesterday. Why was that?"

Martin looked surprised at the question.

"Well, poor chap, it would be a bit tough for him to have to fend for himself, wouldn't it? I thought one of us should rally round," he said.

"I want to see young Mackenzie," said Patrick. "I know he has a tobacconist's shop in Clapham, and he may be in the yellow pages, but it will save me a lot of time if you'll tell me where to find him, or better still, come with me and vouch for me."

"Why do you want to see him? What is all this?" asked Martin.

"How much do you know about his mother's death?" asked Patrick.

"Not a lot. It was very sudden, and it wasn't due to a heart attack or anything like that. Mackenzie is sure she wouldn't have committed suicide. It seems to be a thorough puzzle," Martin said.

"I suppose you haven't seen your parents since the inquest?"

"No. I brought Mackenzie back—he was pretty cut up, and I had a few drinks with him. Then I got involved with my own troubles and I forgot about it," Martin said.

"I don't know how fit you're feeling now," said Patrick, "and what you can manage to take in."

"Oh, I'm better," Martin assured him. "That brew of yours was magical." He gave Patrick a twisted grin. "I don't know why you're so bothered about poor Mrs. Mackenzie, but I might have gassed myself or jumped in the river if you hadn't turned up. So thanks for coming."

"Oh, no," said Patrick firmly. "You were in far too fragile a state to have done either. By the time you felt stronger, you would no longer have wanted to take such a step." He fixed the young man with a steady gaze from behind his spectacles and added, "Don't feast on despair. There's always a more positive alternative. You can do something, 'hope, wish day come, not choose not to be'. I suggest that now you listen while I tell you what has been discovered about the events leading up to the death of Mrs. Mackenzie. Then, if you agree, we will go and see Alec Mackenzie. I'll tell you why on the way, and after that you can tell me about your own misfortunes, if you would care to do so." By that time they will have shrunk to much more endurable proportions, Patrick thought to himself.

"Why are you so interested?" Martin asked.

"Because I'm insatiably curious," Patrick replied. "And

also, more creditably, I'm concerned for your cousin Cathy, for whom all this is being a shattering experience. I want to hurry things on a bit, if I can. The police, inevitably, have to move slowly to build up their case."

"Their case?"

"Their case," Patrick repeated. "This is murder."

Martin stood up.

"Let's have some more coffee, while you fill me in," he said. "First I'll ring up the office and tell them I won't be in today. I'd better go down to my parents after we've seen Mackenzie. I may be needed."

Patrick was pleased to see Gerard Manley Hopkins' advice being so speedily followed. He put the kettle on while Martin telephoned, reflecting that he had spent a great deal of time in other people's kitchens during the past few days.

"I'm for the sack, I should think," said Martin, returning. He looked quite cheerful about it. "I suppose I can sell the house, now Sandra isn't here to need it." He looked about the pretty gay kitchen. "It all cost a packet," he said. "She wouldn't settle for a flat. In spite of the mortgage, it should clear my debts. Well, begin, Dr. Grant. I'm listening."

Patrick complied. He started at the beginning, with Mrs. Ludlow having her dinner in bed, Phyllis dividing the lemon meringue pie into four, and she and Cathy setting forth for the Stable House.

"Afterwards, you can tell me what time you got to Pantons, whom you saw and what happened," he said to Martin.

Martin listened quietly while Patrick went on to describe Sunday morning: how Mrs. Ludlow had rung her bell and Cathy had discovered Mrs. Mackenzie. He told Martin nothing about Phyllis meeting a man for tea in the Cobweb Café, an encounter he had witnessed by chance and that might not be relevant, nor did he refer to the letter to Tim that he had discovered. Martin did not interrupt. He sat appalled. Finally Patrick told him why he wanted to see Alec Mackenzie.

"But why did you come here? Why didn't you go straight to Clapham?" Martin asked.

"I wanted to form an opinion of you," said Patrick bluntly, and when Martin asked no question about that opinion, his estimate of the young man rose.

"Have I time for a quick bath?" asked Martin.

"Oh yes," said Patrick. They might in any case be too early to find out what he wanted to know, but he hoped to get away before Inspector Foster's men came to see Martin, as they were bound to, ultimately.

While Martin was in the bathroom, Patrick, heaving a resigned sigh, started to clear up the squalid evidence of the previous night's thrash that was left all over the sitting-room. Carrying glasses and brimming ashtrays out to the kitchen, he felt very domesticated and wished that Robert, his scout, could see him.

The telephone bell interrupted his smug musings, and he called out to Martin that he would answer it.

It might be Sandra, repentant.

But it wasn't. It was Gerald Ludlow, who sounded very surprised when Patrick announced his identity.

"Your nephew's in the bath. Can I give him a message?" Patrick asked.

"Please." Gerald's voice became guarded. "Does he know how the prevailing wind blows here?"

"He does," said Patrick.

"The man in charge has been to see me. Everyone concerned is to meet at my house tonight at half-past eight, including Martin."

"I'll tell him," Patrick said.

"He must turn up," said Gerald. "It's mandatory."

"I'll see that he understands," said Patrick.

"Why are you there?" asked Gerald. "I rang his office, but they said he hadn't been in. He's all right, I hope? He won't do anything stupid? That girl wasn't any good, he's well rid of her, we all know it couldn't last."

So Gerald knew that Sandra had gone. That was a swift flight of intelligence.

"He's all right," Patrick said.

"But I don't see why you're there," Gerald repeated.

"I'll tell you this evening," Patrick said. "Good-bye," and he hung up before Gerald could reply.

IV

Gerald stared at the telephone receiver in a bewildered manner before he replaced it. Dr. Grant had not been named by the Inspector as one who should be present this evening; on the other hand, he had been up at the house on Saturday

night, and again yesterday. Cathy seemed attached to him.
What could his interest be in the affair? Surely not Cathy?
Banishing such an idea, Gerald resumed his telephone calls.

When asked by the Inspector to summon all the family
together he had protested.

"If you insist, I must arrange it, I suppose," he said, "but I
can't see how it will help. It must have been some frightful
accident."

"I'd like to believe that you're correct, Mr. Ludlow, but
I'm afraid that isn't so," said the Inspector. "There's a lot
more here than meets the eye. If we can wrap this case up
quickly you'll be spared a lot of painful publicity. I'm sure
you're as anxious as I am that the Yard shouldn't be called
in."

"We must keep the newspapers away," said Gerald.

"As soon as the inquest opens again, they'll be on it," said
the Inspector.

"If your chaps keep on coming to the house the village will
be wondering what's up," Gerald protested. "And Mrs. Bludgen
at the lodge doesn't miss much."

"So I've discovered," said the Inspector. "A very useful
witness, Mrs. Bludgen."

Gerald looked at him sharply.

"Do you know what really happened?" he asked.

"I don't want to say any more just now," said the Inspector
primly. "Please just do as I ask. It will make less of a stir
among the members of your family if you arrange it, rather
than me."

"Oh, I agree," said Gerald hastily. "It's all like some dreadful nightmare," he added. "If you're right, whoever did it
must have been out of their mind."

"Maybe," said the Inspector. "It's a difficult case. We've
had to make a lot of inquiries outside this area to get the
background, so it's taken time. The sooner it's all cleared up
the better."

"That's true, at least," said Gerald. "You won't need my
daughter, will you? Nor my wife. They aren't concerned, and
besides, someone must stay with my mother."

"The young lady need not come, but your wife's presence
will be required, sir, if you please," said the Inspector. "And
your two nephews."

"Oh, surely not, Inspector! Martin hasn't been down here
for weeks. And Timothy's only just returned from Spain."

"Would it surprise you to learn that Mr. Martin Ludlow's wife has left him? And that he is heavily in debt? Also that he was seen to enter and leave the grounds of Pantons on Saturday night?" inquired the Inspector heavily.

"Oh no! It can't be true," exclaimed Gerald, but it was the third of these pieces of information that seemed incredible.

"It is true, I assure you. I've just had the report from London. Mrs. Sandra Ludlow left Heathrow early this morning with a gentleman, not her husband; rather older, I believe." The Inspector coughed. "Mr. Martin Ludlow has been a constant loser at a Soho gaming club, and a witness saw him drive through the gates of Pantons on Saturday. I think you'll agree that his position is far from satisfactory, under the circumstances?"

Because of this conversation and its revelations, Martin had been the first person summoned by Gerald to the Inspector's meeting. He telephoned his brother Derek next, and got snapped at for the interruption.

"I've got a lot on," he said. "Can't spare time to talk to you now. That damned Inspector's been on the line already this morning. Why can't they get on and clear this business up? Woman must have committed suicide, it stands to reason."

Gerald did not care for all this indiscreet talk on the telephone, especially from Derek, whose office had a switchboard manned by a girl who might listen in when she had nothing else to do.

"There are a few queries, it seems," he said. "We're all to come, your boys too."

"Good heavens, what a waste of time," said Derek. "It's got nothing to do with them."

"Nevertheless, they're to come," said Gerald. Derek clearly had no notion of Martin's troubles. He would learn about them soon enough.

"You'll tell Betty and Tim?"

"Ring them for me, would you, Gerald? I've got such a lot on, and you know what Betty is. Yackety-yack. I simply haven't the time. You're at home, I gather?"

"Yes. Someone has to be, there's a bit too much going on," said Gerald. "I'll ring Betty."

"Keep her calm," Derek said.

"I'll do my best."

"Right. Sorry I can't talk," Derek said. "See you tonight."

Helen came into the hall as Gerald finished this conversation.

"Derek's pretty fed up about coming round tonight," he said. "He seems to be in a flap about something."

"In a flap," repeated Helen. "That's a British expression?"

"Rather outmoded slang, really," said Gerald. "It goes back to the war." He put his arms round her. "Poor darling, what a beginning. A family grilling by the British bobbies."

Helen kissed him.

"They have their job to do, I guess," she said. "Do they know what happened?"

"I don't think so. The Inspector seems to imagine that by getting us all gathered round in a family circle he'll trap one of us into accusing somebody else of wanting to get rid of Mother." His voice was bitter. "It's horrible. I simply can't believe it. Who would do such a thing?"

"I'm sure none of you would," said Helen. "But I don't believe it was suicide, either. Everything points the other way."

"According to the Inspector, none of us is quite as straightforward as we seem," said Gerald. "Ironic, isn't it? You and I thought we had problems. Now there's young Martin. His wife's left him. The police have discovered that he owes a lot of money. Goodness knows what else they've ferreted out."

"They'll tell us, maybe, tonight," said Helen. She turned away from him, shifting a flower in the bowl on the table. "Poor Martin."

"Derek sounded as if he'd all the cares of the world on his back, too," said Gerald. "Still, the sooner the police get all this cleared up, the better. Then we can forget it and make some plans." He drew her close to him. "We'll have another honeymoon," he said.

V

Derek and Betty were the first to arrive at the Stable House that evening. With them came a sulky, unspeaking Timothy; he wore clean grey trousers and a blue sweater, and he had washed his hair, but in no other way had he followed Cathy's advice.

"What is this all about, Gerald?" Betty asked, fluttering into the house ahead of her men. "Surely the police are making a mountain out of a molehill?"

"We'll have to see, won't we?" Gerald said.

"I've read that if anyone takes sedatives who isn't used to them, and then has a drink, it can be fatal," Betty said. "Mrs. Mackenzie liked a drop, I know."

"The police don't seem to think it's quite as simple as that," said Gerald. He looked at his brother interrogatively, to see if Betty knew what was involved.

His brother shrugged.

"Why anticipate?" he said.

"Do you understand what it's all about, Helen?" Betty asked. "It seems a great riddle to me."

"It's horrible," Helen said.

"Poor dear, fancy all this happening when you've only just arrived," Betty said. "What will you think of us all?"

Helen murmured something indistinguishable, and at this moment the door bell rang. It was Martin.

"Martin! What are you doing here? Where's Sandra?" Betty cried. "I didn't know you were coming."

Martin crossed the room and gave his mother a peck on the cheek; he made no attempt to answer her. Then he greeted his father with a mumbled word. Helen, whom he had not met, was introduced, and Gerald suggested everyone could use a drink before the Inspector arrived.

"But I don't understand why you're here, Martin," Betty repeated.

"Oh Mother, do stop making a fool of yourself. Everyone's got to be here, except Gran and Cathy," Tim growled. "Don't you realise, the police think one of us tried to bump Gran off, but Mrs. Mackenzie got the push instead."

Before their eyes, Betty suddenly shrivelled from a plump upstanding figure into a midget. Her face puckered as her body sagged.

"Timothy, how dare you speak to your mother like that," Derek said in a furious voice.

"Is it true? Is what he says true?" whispered Betty.

"I'm afraid it is, dear," Derek said.

"But it can't be!" Betty looked round the room, at her husband, at her brother-in-law, at her sons. "Not one of the family! She looked at Tim, white-faced and mulish, and remembered with shocked clarity what he had wanted on Saturday, and how he had flung away, out of the house, when his request for money was refused. She suddenly began to feel very sick, but then her common sense returned; Tim was moody, ill-tempered, not very clean; but he was not a liar and he was not violent. There were a number of discreditable things she was sure he would be capable of, but murder was not among them. She felt calmer; it could not be Tim. But who, then?

At this point, Phyllis walked in, without ringing; she was flushed, and apologised for being late.

"Is Cathy all right?" Gerald asked.

"Yes. She's upstairs with Mother. They've got the television up there, watching some programme about birds. Cathy'll ring up if Mother gets fretty," Phyllis said. "I simply told Mother I was coming down to see how Helen is managing with Mrs. Bludgen. How are you?" she added, and everybody laughed.

"She's only been the one time," Helen said. "Tomorrow's her day, isn't it? She scares me to bits. All that fierce red hair, and the way she looks at me, trying to figure out why I'm here, I guess. As if I were a being from another planet."

"To her, you probably seem like one," said Phyllis. "I doubt if she's met an American before. She'll be expecting you to behave like someone in a film."

"Don't you think she might have done a line with a G.I. or two, before Bludgen appeared and swept her off her feet?" Gerald asked. "Whisky, Phyl?"

"Thanks, I'd love one." Phyllis exchanged a smile with Gerald as he gave her her drink; that afternoon, with Helen, they had sat in the garden talking for nearly two hours, discussing the situation in which they found themselves, Mrs. Ludlow's temperament, Cathy's future, and many other things, and Phyllis had experienced a renewal of the deep affection she had always felt for her younger brother. He had suffered a terrible blow when his first wife died; he deserved to be happy with his Helen, if only they could surmount this ill-starred start.

"Phyllis, do you know what this meeting's all about?" Betty quavered. "Derek says the police suspect one of us of—oh, I can't say it! It isn't possible," she finished.

"Yes, it does seem impossible," Phyllis agreed. She spoke calmly. "And in that case, we've nothing to fear, have we? If none of us did this dreadful thing, the police can't prove that we did. We have only to speak the truth."

"Hmph. Yes. Quite so," said Derek. He was the head of the family, if anyone else could be so described while their mother lived. He looked round at them all. "Phyl's right. Everyone simply stick to the truth, and refuse to get rattled. There's nothing to fear. We don't go in for third degree over here."

Helen made a wry face at this, and Gerald filled up his brother's glass again.

"I can't imagine what really happened," he said. "But murder's out of the question."

But was it?

Martin's glass was empty too. Wretched young man, no one had mentioned his misfortunes. Gerald thought that Helen and he were the only people present who knew of them.

They all heard the sound of the police car arriving outside. Its door slammed, and Gerald went to meet the Inspector before he had time to ring. If this scene had to be played, at least let civilised conduct prevail for as long as it could.

Inspector Foster entered the room where all the others were assembled, with the panache of a leading actor making his entrance after the first minutes of a play. He carried a sheaf of papers, and was followed by Sergeant Smithers, who held only a notebook.

"Please sit down, ladies and gentlemen," said the Inspector. He took up a position in front of the hearth, from where he could see them all, ranged round in a semicircle. Obediently, those who already had chairs sat down again. Gerald asked Martin to fetch some more chairs from the kitchen, and finally everyone was disposed. Gerald and Helen were together on the sofa; Tim perched on a tapestry-covered stool in front of the walnut bureau. Betty, in a tub chair near the window, cast a frightened glance at Derek who frowned at her, and shook his head, leaving her more bewildered even than before.

"Well then, is everybody comfortable?" asked Inspector Foster, adopting now the guise of a genial schoolmaster. "I regret that it has been necessary to ask you all to come here this evening, but I am sure you agree that we want to solve this mystery as soon as possible, and with the minimum publicity. I know that Mrs. Ludlow senior is old and frail, and you don't want her worried more than is unavoidable, so the sooner we pool our knowledge, the better." He paused, and gazed at his audience. Betty shuffled in her seat and looked at the carpet. Tim stared at his bitten nails. Martin clasped and unclasped his hands. Derek stared truculently back at the Inspector. Helen and Gerald looked briefly at each other and then past the Inspector's ankles and at the empty grate. Phyllis looked at the red-haired Sergeant, upright on his kitchen chair in an unobtrusive position, pencil and notebook at the ready.

Inspector Foster cleared his throat. His sharp brown eyes seemed to dart about as he surveyed them. Met in a pub or on the racecourse or in some other non-official capacity, he might have seemed an amiable enough acquaintance, Gerald thought, but now he was menacing. He wished the fellow would get on with it.

"By now you are all aware that Mrs. Joyce Mackenzie's death last Saturday night or in the early hours of Sunday morning was not due to natural causes," he began. "She died of an overdose of barbiturates, combined with alcohol, and my purpose is to discover how she came to take these substances." He paused, and shuffled his papers. No one else moved.

"I have spoken to each of you individually about your movements on Saturday night," he went on. "Most of you I saw straight away on Sunday, or on the following day; Mr. Martin Ludlow I met this afternoon. I have taken no statement, however, from Mr. Timothy Ludlow. You," he added, speaking to Tim directly, "did not return from your holiday until Saturday evening. Is that correct?"

"That's right, Inspector," Betty chipped in.

"Please let your son speak for himself, Mrs. Ludlow," said the Inspector, but he did not wait for Timothy to answer. "I have here copies of the statements you have all made and signed concerning the last hours of Mrs. Mackenzie and the whereabouts of you all at that time. Now, some of you may be puzzled about the nature of these inquiries, so I will just go over what happened, as far as we know it.

"On Saturday night Mrs. Ludlow senior took dinner in bed. This was quite usual, I understand?" Here he paused, and looked at Phyllis.

"My mother often has a tray in bed when she is tired," said Phyllis.

"That night it would be reasonable for everyone to assume that Mrs. Ludlow would be tired, for the previous day had been strenuous, with the excitement of a family party," said the Inspector, and he bowed towards Helen, who remained motionless. "It would therefore have been surprising if Mrs. Ludlow had not gone to bed for dinner on Saturday night."

He looked round again, and there were nods from Betty and from Phyllis confirming that this was a fair assumption.

"Now, Mrs. Medhurst, may we hear from you, please, how Mrs. Ludlow's meal was served to her that night?" asked the Inspector.

"I took it up to her, on a tray," said Phyllis.

"Course by course, as she was ready, or how?"

"No, all at once. There was cold soup, chicken fricassee, and her pudding."

"You mean the hot dish was served together with the rest?"

"Yes. My mother has a special plate with a container below it for hot water, to keep her food warm. It irritates her to have someone coming in and out while she is eating, and perhaps finding her not ready for the next course. My mother is very independent, Inspector; she likes to set her own pace and she enjoys her food."

"I see. And so the sweet course was on the tray too, when you took it up?"

"That is so."

"And you served it, Mrs. Medhurst?"

"Yes. I cut up the pie in the kitchen some time earlier. Cathy and I wanted to have our meal promptly because we were coming down here to spend the evening," Phyllis said.

"So there was a period of time in which a piece of pie clearly intended for Mrs. Ludlow was set aside from the rest, in the kitchen?"

"A short time, yes."

"And who could have known that, besides yourself?"

"Anyone who was in the house. In this case, only my niece and Mrs. Mackenzie. We always do it like this when the pudding is a cold one. All the family knows that mother's helping is prepared first," said Phyllis. "Often, if it's trifle or a mousse, or something of that kind, it's made in a separate glass."

"So that if anyone called at the house in the short time between your dividing of the pie, and when you took the tray up to your mother, they would have known where to find your mother's portion?"

"Yes, *if* anyone called," said Phyllis.

"And you went up the staircase with the tray, or did you go in the lift?"

"I used the stairs."

"I see. Thank you. Now, Mr. Ludlow." Inspector Foster turned to Derek. "I put it to you that you called on your mother on Saturday evening," he said.

Derek stiffened in his seat and stared fiercely back at the Inspector.

"Certainly not," he said at once. "I was at home all the evening."

Inspector Foster turned to a paper that he held in his hand.

"Before you say anything more, Mr. Ludlow, I must tell you that you were seen arriving at Pantons at a quarter to seven that evening, and were observed leaving again twenty minutes later."

There was silence. Everyone gaped at Derek, and Betty gave a little moan.

"That Bludgen woman!" Derek exploded. "She does nothing but watch her window all day long."

"Mr. Ludlow, would you care to change your remark about visiting Pantons on Saturday evening?" the Inspector asked in a mild voice.

"I did come up. I just popped in to see mother for a few minutes," Derek said, very red in the face now.

"And will you tell us why you called?" asked the Inspector smoothly.

"No, I won't. It's none of your damned business," Derek said.

"Mr. Ludlow, I suggest that you wanted your mother to lend or give you a considerable sum of money, and that she refused," said the Inspector. "Think, before you reply." He waited, pencil in the air, like the conductor of an orchestra with his baton raised, while Derek gasped and spluttered, and finally subsided.

"I don't know how you've found out, but it's true," he said at last.

Betty uttered a small cry. She stared from her husband to Tim, appalled, and at Martin, then back to Derek once again.

"And did your mother consent to your request?"

"She did not," said Derek heavily. "I expect you've already asked her."

"No. I have been hoping to spare Mrs. Ludlow from too much distress," said the Inspector. "Will you tell us why you wanted the money?"

"I'm sure you already know the answer to that," said Derek, with heavy irony.

"I should like to hear it from you, sir, if you please," said the Inspector.

"I'm not obliged to tell you," Derek said, fiery again. "I should consult my solicitor first."

"Very well." Inspector Foster inclined his head. "As you wish. Nevertheless, you admit that you visited your mother on Saturday evening?"

The atmosphere in the room had altered during this interchange. Everyone was looking now at Derek. Gerald sat forward, tense, and Phyllis gripped the arms of her chair. Martin and Tim looked shocked, and their mother covered her face with her hand. Helen, solemn-faced, gazed at Derek for a brief instant and then glanced away.

"I admit it," Derek said. "But I didn't go fiddling about with her supper tray, if that's what you're implying."

"Derek, don't lose your temper," Phyllis warned.

"I object to all this nosey-parkering," Derek stormed.

"So do we all, but we must put up with it till this thing's sorted out," said Phyllis.

"Very wise, Mrs. Medhurst," said the Inspector. He turned to Derek again. "Now sir, be calm, please. Whom did you see at Pantons that night, apart from your mother?"

Derek seemed about to explode again, but he thought better of it, and answered with an attempt at calmness.

"No one. I could hear my sister and Mrs. Mackenzie talking in the kitchen. I didn't see Cathy, but the wireless was on in her room. I expect she was in there," Derek said. "I slipped in and out quietly. I didn't want to be long, nor to explain why I had come. I left my car down the drive."

"You left yours down there too, hidden among the bushes, didn't you, sir?" the Inspector now said, turning to Martin, who had been watching his father in a horrified way during this conversation. "Will you account for your presence at Pantons that night, please?"

Martin nodded glumly.

"It's a long story," he said. "Put briefly, I'd been gambling pretty heavily and lost. I owe about two thousand pounds."

"Martin!" This from Betty.

"You may as well know it all. I was afraid of losing Sandra. She'd met a chap who was loaded. I won a bit at first, but then there came a landslide," Martin said.

"You saw your grandmother and she refused to lend you any money?" said the Inspector.

"Exactly. She said she'd given us a generous wedding present to help buy the house, which was true, and we couldn't expect any more."

"And what time did you call?"

"I'm sure the redoubtable Mrs. Bludgen has told you that," said Martin. "I arrived at about twenty past seven." He looked at his father. "We must have just missed each other," he added, with a faint smile.

"But you did not leave until nine-fifteen," said the Inspector. "Why was that?"

"I didn't go to see Grandmother straight away. I walked about in the garden for ages, trying to think of some other way to get the money," Martin said. "But I'd already tried everything else. The house is fully mortgaged as it is."

"So both you, Mr. Martin Ludlow, and you, Mr. Derek Ludlow, had the opportunity and the motive to take some capsules from the parcel in the hall, and secrete the powder they contained in the slice of pie prepared for Mrs. Ludlow senior," said the Inspector.

"How could they, Inspector?" Gerald burst out. "Do you mean to say that either my brother or my nephew went into the kitchen and under the nose of Mrs. Mackenzie introduced sleeping pills into some food? Impossible."

"Mrs. Mackenzie may have left the kitchen briefly," said the Inspector. "The murderer had only to wait for that to happen, hiding in the lift, perhaps. If the capsules were opened, and the powder taken out of the gelatine containers, it would not have taken long to insert it in the meringue part of the pie. Any spilt powder would resemble sugar."

Tim sat up and seemed about to speak, but Martin intervened.

"Well, which of us was it, Inspector? Who's your fancy? My father or me? Take your choice," he said.

"Oh Martin, stop it," Phyllis said. "This is nonsense. Of course you didn't do it, and nor did Derek."

"You're sure of that, are you, Mrs. Medhurst?" asked the Inspector. "Why?"

"Of course I'm sure. Derek is my brother. I know him," Phyllis said. "And I've known Martin since he was a baby. It's impossible."

"It's not impossible. You may think it unlikely, but I have

demonstrated that both Mr. Ludlow and his son had the motive and the opportunity to arrange this crime," said the Inspector. "There was, however, someone else with equal motive, and far better opportunity." Here he paused, and looked at Phyllis, who returned his gaze steadily.

"Mrs. Medhurst, you have declared that neither your nephew nor your brother did this thing. Are you so convinced of this because in fact you know who did it? Because you did it yourself?"

"Inspector, no! I protest!" cried Gerald, starting forward. "You go too far."

"No, Gerald." Phyllis held up her hand. "Don't stop the Inspector. I think we must hear what he has to say."

She sat back in her chair, her hands clasping its arms and her legs neatly crossed at the ankle. Though she looked relaxed, her whole body was taut. Derek, now that the immediate attack had moved from him, became slightly less red in the face but he looked at the Inspector as though he spoke in a foreign language, so alien did his theorising seem. Betty had almost abandoned hope of following what was said; she sat in her little chair plucking at her skirt with her fingers and occasionally glancing round at the others. Tim had stopped biting his nails; he looked white and shocked. Martin watched the Inspector intently; once, he looked at the clock that stood on the mantelpiece and was amazed to find that it was already nine o'clock. Helen sat twisting the sapphire and diamond ring she wore on her left hand; she looked at Phyllis. In the background Sergeant Smithers seized the chance of a lull in the talk to look up from his notebook and cast a quick glance round the room.

"Mrs. Medhurst," the Inspector resumed. "It's true to say, is it not, that your mother treats you with some lack of sympathy?"

"My mother is old, crippled, and often in pain, Inspector. She does not mean to be unkind," said Phyllis sharply.

"But if you wished to marry again, your mother would object?"

Now everyone stared at Phyllis; their faces, except for Helen's, clearly revealed that such a possibility was outside their wildest speculations.

"If such a position arose, my mother would certainly try to prevent it," Derek mumbled at last, when it was obvious that his sister either would not, or could not, speak. He cleared his throat. "The way she treats Phyllis—my sister—is disgraceful, and we have been very much at fault in allowing it to happen."

Phyllis found her tongue.

"Derek, why bother to reply to such a stupid question?" she said. "This whole discussion seems to be entirely made of 'ifs.'"

Inspector Foster consulted a paper in his hand.

"Yesterday morning, Mrs. Medhurst, you had coffee at the Cobweb Café in Fennersham with a Mr. Maurice Richards, of Number Five, The Drive, Fennersham," he said. "You meet this gentleman for tea each Friday afternoon at the same café, and last winter you both attended art classes at the Fennersham Evening Institute. You meet him for coffee on Wednesday mornings when you do your weekly shopping, and you have visited his residence on a number of occasions. Do you deny this?"

Phyllis was now a fiery red.

"That is perfectly true, Inspector," she said, and her hands were tight on the arms of her chair. "But it hardly constitutes a romance."

Her dignity was impressive.

"I put it to you, Mrs. Medhurst, that you wish to marry Mr. Richards. If you were to do so, depriving your mother of your services, she might cut you out of her will, and this would be a matter of resentment after so many years of care. You would naturally prefer your share of her fortune rather than live merely on a bank manager's pension. And so would Mr. Richards."

"Inspector, I refuse to listen to this any longer," Gerald exclaimed, springing to his feet. "I agreed to this meeting in my house because you insisted, and I hoped it might be constructive in some way. But all you have done is to accuse my brother, my nephew, and now my sister of the basest cupidity. My sister is an honourable woman; perhaps you don't meet many of them in your profession. She looks after our mother out of regard for her high sense of duty. She is incapable of the twisted thinking you impute to her."

"I'm sure we all appreciate your family loyalty, Mr. Ludlow," said the Inspector. "But affection blinds the judgement, very often. The facts speak for themselves. Mrs. Medhurst had a strong motive; she had ample opportunity. And she fetched the pills from the chemist's shop, leaving them in the hall in a careless manner that was unusual for her. By leaving them where others could have found them she hoped to confuse the issue. She was, of course, aware that other members of the family had their troubles too."

"Inspector, you're wrong." Tim was on his feet now. "Aunt Phyllis wouldn't do a thing like that. You don't know everything." He ran his fingers wildly through his hair. "I was here that night, too," he began desperately, and Phyllis interrupted.

"Shut up, Tim," she said peremptorily.

"Yes, shut up, Tim," said a brisk new voice.

Tim, startled, turned towards the door, and even the Inspector now looked taken aback as into the room came Patrick Grant. He was followed by a pale young man with a haggard expression.

"Forgive me, Inspector, for intruding on your conference," Patrick began. "But it's justified. As most of you know, this is Mr. Alec Mackenzie, whose mother's death is the reason for your presence here tonight."

He crossed the room, followed by the young man, and stopped in front of Helen, who rose slowly from the sofa where she had been sitting.

"Mrs. Ludlow, you have not met Mr. Mackenzie," he said. "Mackenzie, this is Mrs. Gerald Ludlow."

Helen said nothing. Her face was grey. Gerald stood beside her, his bulk against her shoulder. Martin, watching, saw their hands meet. No one spoke.

"Dr. Grant, I must ask you to leave us." Inspector Foster said angrily.

Patrick turned to him.

"I am here because I have something relevant to tell you, Inspector," he said. "I am sure you have been describing very capably what may have happened last Saturday night when Mrs. Joyce Mackenzie unfortunately swallowed a quantity of sodium amytal, and died. You are doubtless convinced, as I confess I was myself at first, that the pills were intended for Mrs. Ludlow senior. The lady possesses a considerable fortune, and sees no reason why her children or grandchildren should receive any part of it before she dies, however much they might need a sum of money now."

As he spoke, Patrick had somehow edged the Inspector away from his position in the centre of the hearth and taken up this place himself. Inspector Foster now stood slightly to one side of him, wearing an outraged expression on his face yet unable to halt the flow of speech. Sergeant Smithers, scribbling fast, longed for a second pair of eyes so as to observe the scene.

Patrick pressed on, giving no one a chance to interrupt him; he had the initial advantage of surprise. Gerald, who had expected after their words on the telephone to see him earlier, had by now forgotten all about him.

"Several members of the Ludlow family are in financial or other difficulties," Patrick said. "Mrs. Ludlow senior is not the gentlest of matriarchs, and doubtless few tears would be shed were she to die peacefully. On Saturday night, for some reason, she did not eat her pudding. Mrs. Mackenzie was well known to possess a sweet tooth and an inability to resist eating up any tit-bits that are left over. Accordingly she finished Mrs. Ludlow's pudding, and she died."

Now Patrick took a step backwards so that he might subject the Inspector to the regard that had quelled many an unruly undergraduate.

"Inspector, I put it to you that the matter of the pudding is merely a coincidence, because the victim all along was intended to be Mrs. Mackenzie," he said.

There was a gasp in the room.

"Dr. Grant, I protest—" the Inspector began, but Patrick went on talking as if he had not uttered.

"The pills may have been in the whisky that Mrs. Mackenzie drank. The murderer could have cleared up such evidence easily enough before the police arrived on Sunday morning," he said.

As the Inspector tried once again to stop him, Patrick raised a hand.

"No, hear me out, Inspector," he continued. "In all puzzles, the best way to find a solution is to look for the unusual. On this occasion there were two unusual things. The first was that Mrs. Mackenzie, a creature of habit, stepped aside from her weekly routine. Each Wednesday and Sunday she posted a letter to her daughter in Winnipeg. Last Saturday she posted an extra letter, or her Sunday one a day early. She must have had a reason.

"I called today on Mr. Alec Mackenzie to find out if his sister had a birthday or anniversary, anything that could be the explanation. He could think of nothing to account for an additional letter. It therefore seemed probable that Mrs.

Mackenzie must have had some special news to tell her daughter."

The Inspector had now given up trying to silence Patrick. Instead, he was listening with attention.

"Now we come to the second unusual event that happened," Patrick said. "Mr. Gerald Ludlow had recently got married. On Friday night he brought his wife to Pantons."

He paused. Helen and Gerald, still close together, stood immobile.

"Letters normally take three or four days to reach Winnipeg from England," Patrick said. "I thought that by today Mrs. Mackenzie's daughter might have received her mother's letter, so, with the assistance of Mr. Mackenzie here, I telephoned to her. The letter has arrived. Mrs. Mackenzie and Mrs. Helen Ludlow had met before."

But before he had finished speaking, Helen had fainted.

VI

The ensuing pandemonium died down eventually. Helen recovered consciousness very quickly and was taken upstairs at once by her husband, with Phyllis in attendance. The remaining Ludlows sat about looking stunned, and when the sound of a door closing indicated that the retreating party could not overhear what passed below, Inspector Foster rounded on Patrick.

"You should have got in touch with me privately," he said. "This alters everything."

"I know," said Patrick blandly. "That's why I hurried down."

The Inspector, making a huge effort, decided to swallow his pride. Time would be lost if he berated Patrick further, pointing out that the telephone service operated between London and Fennersham and making other such caustic comments on his actions.

"What did the letter say?" he asked.

"I'm sorry, Inspector, but I can't tell you that," said Patrick. "It was told to me in confidence. The letter only arrived this morning, and as you know, Winnipeg time is six hours behind ours. Hence part of the delay." He looked at the Inspector consideringly. "Mrs. Mackenzie's daughter was naturally very upset by the letter, coming on top of the news of

her mother's death. I appreciate that I have upset your plans
by turning up like this with such information, but you had to
know."

"Yes. Yes, I did." The Inspector had been thinking rapidly.
Patrick rather admired the way he adjusted so quickly to the
new situation.

"Smithers, we must get back to the station," he said.

"Yes, sir." The Sergeant rose smartly, putting his Biro into
his breast pocket and closing his notebook.

"Mr. Mackenzie, may I ask you to come with us?" the
Inspector said. "We must get on to your sister, and I'm sure
we'll need your help."

Alec Mackenzie mumbled some affirmative.

Patrick said a few words to him in a low voice, and gave
him a brisk pat on the shoulder. Mackenzie managed a wan
smile, and then went with the two policemen towards the
door. Martin followed to see them off. When he came back
his mother was standing in the middle of the room fluttering
her hands in a helpless way.

"What does it mean?" she asked. Her voice was a wail.

Tim, in the background, leaned on the mantelpiece biting
his nails. He paid no attention to anyone else, gazing down at
his scuffed shoes in abstract concentration.

"There was some link between Helen and Mrs. Mackenzie—
in America? But Mrs. Mackenzie came from Canada." This
was Derek, thinking aloud.

"You must hear about it from your brother, not from me,"
said Patrick.

"Did he know?"

"I think you'll find he did."

Betty had given up. The immediate threat that one of her
family might be arrested for something she knew they could
never have done was gone. Meanwhile, near at hand, was
Martin in distress. She put out an arm towards him.

"Tell me about Sandra, dear," she said, and beckoned him
into a corner.

Martin cast a wry glance in Patrick's direction as he allowed
himself to be led away. He had begun to fear, as time went
on and Patrick did not appear, that the Rover must have
failed him, but in fact his arrival was timed perfectly, giving
the Inspector long enough to show his hand completely. It
had been agreed between them that Martin must be punctu-
al, and must pay great attention to all that was said in case

there were points not clear to Patrick afterwards. Excitement had carried Martin through the evening, but now he felt an anti-climax. His mother must be told the worst, though; best get it over, and free his father for the *tête-à-tête* with Patrick that clearly loomed.

"What a kettle of fish," Derek was saying. "I'd like a word, Dr. Grant, if you don't mind."

"Of course." Patrick glanced round the room. "Let's go outside, shall we?"

They walked together out into the cobbled yard. The air was still full of the scent from the geraniums, and overhead a light showed in an upstairs window.

"You arrived just in time to stop Tim confusing the issue," Derek said. "He'd just announced that he was at Pantons on Saturday night. I suppose you realised that I was too?"

"I thought you might have been," said Patrick. As yet he had only surmised that Derek might be in trouble, and that chiefly because Betty was clearly so disturbed, yet could give no reason for her anxiety apart from her normal state of maternal fret.

"Tim's in trouble, of course."

"He is," said Patrick grimly. "But not with the university."

"I wouldn't listen when he asked me for help," said Derek. "I've got this crisis with my business. You'll hear about it. But I should have made time for the boys. Martin's in a mess too."

"Martin, I think, will be able now to dig himself out," said Patrick. "I'll deal with Tim, if you like. On a short-term basis only. I can resolve the immediate difficulty and you can sort him out later. In the end he may profit from a narrow escape from real disaster. I'll keep you posted."

"He may have to leave Oxford," Derek said. "I'm in a real mess. He'll lose his allowance."

"If things are as bad as that, his grant will be adjusted," Patrick said calmly. "It won't hurt him to go short."

"You think Martin can manage? I can't pay off his debts, I've too many of my own."

"His wife has finally gone, so he can sell his assets," Patrick said. "And he hasn't got to pay for her. She was, I gather, expensive."

"Poor boy." Derek spoke sadly. "That must hurt. I never knew what he saw in her. She was pretty, if you like that type. Thin, you know, like a bird. They met winter-sporting, if you please, and married almost at once. Fancy trying to build a marriage on a fortnight's ski-ing holiday."

Patrick forebore to say that it had sometimes been achieved.

"He seems to have been rather unlucky," he said aloud. He was accustomed to harder-hearted young men who would have seen through Sandra at once. From what Martin had told him, it seemed clear that Sandra had rebounded in his direction after an affair that went wrong; she had thought his prospects better than they were, and expected his grandmother to subsidise his perfectly adequate salary right from the start. When she learned that they might expect nothing from the old lady except upon her whim, and that they must meekly visit Pantons every Sunday into the bargain, she soon grew bored with Martin. Because of her job she had a vast number of acquaintances, many of whom admired her; it was not difficult for her to find an alternative.

"I don't know which of us is in the worst pickle," Derek said. "If you hadn't arrived when you did, the Inspector would have made an arrest. I suppose the moment's only been postponed."

"I think you'll find he's been diverted," Patrick said. "Now, shall we go back to the others?" He felt that there was a strong chance of Betty having induced an emotional scene with her sons; however, she was sitting calmly with them both, and they were deciding that Martin would return home with them for the night.

Phyllis came downstairs just after Derek and Patrick went back into the house. She said that Helen was resting, and Gerald was staying with her.

"I was telling Dr. Grant that he came in the nick of time to prevent Inspector Foster charging someone," Derek said to his sister. "I fancy the odds were evenly balanced between you and me."

Phyllis still had the high colour in her cheeks. She gave Derek a wry smile.

"I think I was favourite, by a short head," she said.

"Well, not any more," said Derek flatly.

"No. Things are even worse now," said Phyllis. She faced Patrick. "Inspector Foster will be back to arrest Helen as soon as he's got in touch with Winnipeg." A grim expression crossed her face.

"He won't have much to go on," Patrick said. "Besides, he won't know whether to suspect Helen, or your brother Gerald. They both had the opportunity, and the motive was the same."

"We'll take it as read that there must be some shady event in Helen's past that Mrs. Mackenzie knew about," said Derek. "Allowing for that, how could either she or Gerald have done this thing?"

Patrick said: "When I came here on Saturday evening, I arrived at eight-thirty. Just before that, your brother had been absent for some time, ostensibly fetching ice. He could have been up at Pantons, doping Mrs. Mackenzie's whisky. Everyone seemed to know that she always had a nightcap. He could have slipped up through the garden so as to avoid Mrs. Medhurst and Cathy coming down, and also that would explain why I did not meet him. He could have used the back door and slipped up unseen, or if he did meet Mrs. Mackenzie, he could pretend to be visiting his mother. Mrs. Mackenzie herself would be busy in the kitchen then. It would have been easy for him to remove the bottle containing the drug from her room later, and to exchange the glass by her bed for another. We don't know if it was checked for prints; probably not, since there was no trace of barbiturate in it, but a glass from the cupboard downstairs would be certain to carry Mrs. Mackenzie's prints since she would have put it away."

He paused and looked at Phyllis.

"Your brother did come up to Pantons directly after you found the body?"

"Yes. He was with us in ten minutes," Phyllis said. Her colour had faded now.

"It could have been a joint operation," Patrick said. "Mrs. Helen Ludlow went to fetch some money for my collecting box. She was gone for rather a long time. She could have slipped up to Pantons and put the pills in the whisky then, and her husband could have cleared up later."

"Helen wouldn't have known the way," said Derek. "The house was strange to her. She wouldn't have known where Mrs. Mackenzie's room was."

"She and Gerald went up to see Mother on Friday night, after you'd gone home," said Phyllis heavily. "She would have known. But I'm sure they had nothing to do with it, whatever you say, Dr. Grant. I wish you hadn't interfered. It would have been better if Inspector Foster had arrested me. He wouldn't have been able to prove anything against me in the end, the whole thing is circumstantial. Now look what's happening to Gerald and Helen."

"People do strange things for love, Mrs. Medhurst," Patrick said. "You seem willing to be charged with a crime you did not commit in order to spare your brother. Might he not have been capable of carrying it out to protect the woman he loves?"

"But what from?" said Betty. "What had she done?"

"I think I'd better tell you," Phyllis said. She looked at Patrick, but he gave her no help. "Yes," she decided. "You'll have to know. Then you'll realise what we're up against. But it must never be mentioned to anyone else, unless in the end it becomes public knowledge. Is that understood? Boys?"

Martin and Timothy nodded. Martin already knew what was coming, since he had been with Patrick and Alec Mackenzie during the long telephone conversation with Canada.

"I'm not certain of dates and places," Phyllis said. "But briefly it was like this. Helen, as we know, was married before. She was moderately happy for a year or so. Then she had a baby—a little girl. After that, her husband changed; he seemed to turn against her, he resented the baby, and he started to drink a lot—he'd always been a heavy drinker, but Helen had hoped he'd change when they were married."

"Many a foolish girl has been caught like that," said Derek dryly. "Sorry, Phyl. Go on."

"Her husband lost his job, on account of the drinking, and they moved around a bit, but he never kept any job for long, and Helen couldn't go out to work because of the baby, who was delicate. Her husband thought there was nothing wrong with it, and that it was just Helen making a fuss, but the baby died. It had some heart trouble—they might have been able to put it right nowadays, this was all about ten years ago. Anyway, things got worse than ever after this, and Helen eventually left her husband. After a long time—some years—she met someone else, and they were going to get married. Helen got a divorce—it's quite easy over there, and she didn't have any trouble about that. But her husband found where she was living with this other man, in a lakeside hut somewhere in Ontario. The other man was a Canadian. Her husband turned up, and beat up this man. Helen was there when it happened. She said that by this time her husband was on drugs. She was involved in the fighting. Her husband got hit on the head and fell off the little jetty into the lake. As he was unconscious, he drowned. Helen went to gaol for manslaughter and that's where she met Mrs. Mackenzie."

"What! In prison?" The gasp came from Betty.

Phyllis nodded.

"Mrs. Mackenzie was in for stealing. She'd been working for some rich family and had been taking money that was left lying about, and jewellery. Her son Alec was very ill, and she needed it. There's no welfare state over there."

"Mrs. Mack pinching the spoons! No, I can't believe it," Derek said.

"It's true. She made Alec come over to England when she was sentenced. There were some relations over here who helped him get started. She followed later. She's been perfectly honest ever since, I'm certain," said Phyllis. "It's a bit of a shock, isn't it? But it adds up. Canada's a big place, but to start again Mrs. Mack thought she'd better come home, and Helen went back to America."

"What happened to the other man? Helen's—er—the other man?" asked Martin. Young Mackenzie's sister had not given them as clear an account as this on the telephone.

"He died as a result of the brawl. The police found Helen with a stick in her hand covered in blood and hair from her husband's head. That was what finished it for her. The other man probably struck the fatal blow, but he was dead and couldn't say so, and Helen was too shocked to be able to help herself. She said she didn't care what happened, she simply wanted to die. She was lucky not to be charged with murder!"

"Murder!" The word, uttered on a sigh by Betty, shivered round the room.

"What a perfectly ghastly story," Derek said. "Did Gerald know all this?"

"Yes, she told him right away, when he started to get serious about her. That was why she didn't want to marry him. She says she brings bad luck to the people she loves," said Phyllis. "It seems to be true."

Patrick said: "Look, let's all help ourselves to some of your brother's whisky. I'm sure he won't mind. And then we'll just think about this quietly." He crossed to the tray where Gerald had set out the bottles earlier, and began liberally handing out drinks all round. Martin helped him. Everyone was silent, stunned by what they had heard.

"Now then," said Patrick. "As I see it, your sister-in-law Helen Ludlow has had a most unlucky life so far, but she is not a proven murderer. She was involved in a violent situation which she did not provoke. The man she loved and the man she feared both died; neither could describe the fight. A good lawyer might have got her off any charge, but as Mrs. Medhurst has said, she was beyond caring, and she went to prison. Years later, when she hopes that all this could be forgotten, she meets on the other side of the world a woman who can reveal her past. A chance in a million. Those are the facts." He puffed away at his pipe.

"Mrs. Mackenzie could have told Grandmother and ruined Helen's chance of a new life," said Martin slowly.

"Helen could also have ruined Mrs. Mackenzie's reputation," Patrick said. "She might have lost her job."

"That could account for suicide!" Phyllis snatched at this straw. "Mrs. Mackenzie might have thought Helen's position was the stronger one. She might have been afraid for Alec—the disgrace, if it got out. I presume he never knew what happened?"

"No. His sister is the elder. She saw to getting him off, over to England. They made out that Mrs. Mackenzie had T.B. and had to go to a sanatorium. He heard the truth today for the first time."

"Poor young man." This was Betty.

Phyllis had no time to spare for pity outside the family.

"Gerald will be down soon," she said. "We ought to go. We can't discuss it here like this. I'm certain Helen is innocent, and if either she or Gerald is arrested I shall tell the Inspector I knew all about this business."

"Ah, but when did you learn?" asked Patrick. "Just now, upstairs? Or earlier?"

"That's my affair," said Phyllis brusquely.

"You've always had a soft spot for Gerald, haven't you, Phyl?" said Derek rather wistfully.

"There's Cathy to be thought of, too," said Betty. She seemed to have recovered some of her self-control.

"Yes. Quite right, my dear," said Derek. He patted her shoulder absently. "You'd better know the worst," he said. "We're in real trouble with the business. Fifty thousand pounds of clients' money has disappeared."

"Dad!"

"Derek!"

Betty and Martin spoke together. Tim remained silent; his

ears had received so many shocks in the last minutes that he was almost unable to absorb any more.

"Oh, I haven't been embezzling the clients' money," Derek said. "But someone has, and I'm responsible. I'm the senior partner, and I've been negligent."

So that was it. Patrick, in an odd way, felt quite relieved for Betty's sake that the trouble was not another woman. Looking at her face, he saw that she was, too.

"Don't tell Gerald yet. Poor fellow, he's got enough on his plate as it is," said Derek. "But I was hanged if I was going to tell that policeman. Let him find out for himself what he doesn't know already. He seems to have got wind of it, as it is."

It might have been bluff on the Inspector's part, thought Martin. Or could someone in his father's office have said something outside?

"We'd better go home," said Betty. Her face looked piteous. "Then you can tell us what we're going to do."

"Yes," agreed Derek. "We can't do anything here before the morning. You'll stay and see Gerald, Phyl?"

"Yes. If he doesn't come down, I'll go upstairs again," she said.

"Tell him not to worry too much," said Derek vaguely.

They straggled out of the room, Tim last. Patrick put out a hand and held him back.

"Just a minute, Timothy," he said, and drew from his pocket a letter which he handed to the boy.

"Yours, I think. Come and see me about it tomorrow morning, early. I'll expect you at my sister's house at eight. The matter seems to be urgent, and we're going to be busy."

VII

It was nearly eleven o'clock when Phyllis opened the front door of Pantons and went quietly into the house. All was still. She looked into each downstairs room to make sure it was empty before she went upstairs. How had Derek and Martin managed to slip past her on Saturday night without being seen? She felt foolish as she opened the lift door in case it held a concealed intruder, but her nerves were on edge and she did not know from which direction to expect the next blow.

There was a light showing under Cathy's door, so she knocked gently and went in.

Cathy was lying flat on her back in bed with a book held above her nose.

"Cathy dear, you'll go blind reading at that angle," said her aunt.

Cathy put the book down on her stomach and blinked at Phyllis, slowly returning to the present day from the time of the Jacobites.

"It stops you getting a crick in your neck," she said. "This is one of your library books. I took it from your room, I hope you don't mind?"

"That's all right, dear," said Phyllis.

"It's blissfully soppy," Cathy said. "Just the thing for now, after all the gloom."

"Did you manage all right this evening? No storms with your grandmother?"

"No. She was O.K.," said Cathy. She struggled up into a sitting position. "We played cards for a bit, and I read to her. That book's pretty terrible. Does she really enjoy it?"

"I don't think she listens," said Phyllis. "I think it's the sound of a voice that she likes. Did she take a pill?"

"She had her red one. She wouldn't take a sleeping pill," said Cathy. "I coped all right with her bodily needs. Golly!" She made a wry face at the memory. "I wouldn't be a nurse for anything. But it was worse for Gran. Do you know, I really believe she was embarrassed."

"You'll both get used to it," Phyllis said. They must.

"We'll never find anyone else like Mrs. Mack, willing to turn her hand to anything," Cathy lamented.

"I'm inclined to agree," said her aunt.

"Perhaps we should get a nurse? It would mean more liberty."

"We won't think about it now. One thing at a time," said Phyllis.

"How did you get on with the cops? Was it grisly?"

"It was rather," said Phyllis.

"Did it do any good? Did the murderer blench and confess?" Flippancy masked her true concern.

"Of course not," said Phyllis shortly. "There isn't one. The Inspector put forward various ideas, but he was only guessing. In the end he gave up. I don't think we'll ever know what really happened." Time enough for Cathy to hear more the next day. It was late, and she was too tired to know what to say for the best.

"Your friend Dr. Grant turned up," she said.

"Oh, did he?" Cathy brightened. Patrick would tell her the details; it was only fair in return for all she had told him. By this time she knew he was totally gripped by the puzzle. "Why did he come?"

"He seems to consider himself almost one of the family," said Phyllis. "He brought Alec Mackenzie with him."

"Oh. Poor chap, having to be there. It must have been horrid."

"Yes," said Phyllis. "And totally unnecessary. He looked a bit green. Well, I'm for bed, my dear. Good night. Don't read too late." She bent and kissed Cathy, as she had done most nights of her life for the last eleven years except during absence at school.

"Good night, Aunt Phyl. Sleep well," said Cathy.

Her aunt left the room, and she slid down under the sheet again and picked up her book. Soon she was back in an underground passage below a gaunt Cornish mansion, where a girl like herself was trapped while the incoming tide dripped through a hole in the tunnel, and her lover, above, galloped his horse through the night to her rescue.

Phyllis paused outside her mother's door. There was no sound, and the light was out. The old lady must be asleep, or she would have called out when he heard Phyllis return; her ears were still exceedingly sharp. Phyllis went back to her own room and prepared for bed.

When she was ready, she went to the window and leaned out. It was very quiet outside; not even an owl broke the silence, and no night breeze stirred the trees. Her mother's window, like the rest of the house, was dark. Phyllis stayed there for a while, smoking a last cigarette and brooding; then she got into bed where she read for some time in an effort to reach a state of tranquillity, but the book failed to hold her, and she felt no calmer.

Eventually she opened a drawer in her bedside table, took out a blue capsule and swallowed it down with some water from the glass already beside her.

Along the corridor, Mrs. Ludlow leaned against her pillows; she always slept in an upright position. Her light was out, and she could see beyond the pale square of her window the glow from Phyllis's room. She knew that Phyllis would be

smoking and reading; mooning, Mrs. Ludlow called it. She
had been very late coming back from Gerald's. Popping down
for a minute, indeed. Mrs. Ludlow had known how it would
be, and had said as much to Cathy. She had thought of calling
to Phyllis when she heard her at the door, but had decided
against it. Later, if she could not sleep, Phyllis should be
summoned.

She thought about her children in their youth. Derek had
always been solemn and plodding, Phyllis dull. Gerald was
lively enough, though; she remembered him doing tricks on
his bicycle, riding his pony bareback at top speed round the
paddock, playing rugby for his school, and then going off to
the war, slim, serious, bright-eyed, in his khaki, and so like
his father. He was heavier now, fatter, twenty years older
than his father had been when he died.

Her mind went blank and she drifted into a little sleep, but
presently woke with a start. Something unpleasant had happened. She lay trying to remember what it could be. At last
she thought of Mrs. Mackenzie.

What a lot of red tape there was nowadays. All those
policemen tramping about making a fuss over what was a
straightforward matter. It was annoying, though, to think that
a replacement must be found. Phyllis could quite well manage alone, with perhaps more help for the cleaning, but she
seemed to think she could not; her jaunts to the library and
her hair-do's gave her ideas. Well, there would be no more
art classes; Mrs. Ludlow could not be left with someone she
did not know on Tuesday nights.

Of course, Helen might come. That was a happy inspiration.

She dozed again, but she did not really feel ready for sleep
and soon woke, her mind active, burrowing back and forth
through the years. She played with images of Gerald in his
pedal car, charging across the lawn uttering "Brrm-brrm"
roaring sounds from his throat. Then Phyllis, in a white
muslin dress with a blue sash, her long, fair hair kept back by
an Alice band, off to a party; she held her red velvet cloak
over her arm, and wore a pair of bronze pumps with elastic
crossed over her insteps. "Hold your stomach in, child. Put
your shoulders back," her mother had said to her sternly.
"You're far too fat." Across the years, Mrs. Ludlow remembered; saw again, too, the sudden bright colour in Phyllis's
cheeks; she could still make it rise with a word.

Phyllis's window was dark now. She must be asleep. She

should have just a little while longer. Mrs. Ludlow, meanwhile, lay musing, thinking of not very much most of the
time, but sometimes of the long days of her courtship, and
then back to her childhood, with vague memories of her
kind, indulgent father with his curly grey beard and smell of
tobacco; and of a faded pale stranger, lavender-scented, whom
she saw each evening: her invalid mother.

At half-past two she rang her bell.

It pealed shrilly in Phyllis's room. She woke up slowly,
with a thick taste in her mouth and a great reluctance to
return to consciousness. The bell pealed on.

Phyllis blundered about, found her slippers at last and put
on her dressing-gown. It was so long since her mother had
had any sort of attack in the night that she never expected
one now; some years back Mrs. Ludlow had had a very slight
heart attack, so mild that it left no trace. It was almost
forgotten.

The bell still rang as Phyllis opened her bedroom door.
She felt doped from the pill she had taken, and wove her way
crookedly down the passage. If that ringing went on, Cathy
would wake.

Mrs. Ludlow had switched on her light when she decided
to ring for Phyllis. She waited impatiently, twitching at the
bedclothes with one knobbled hand and clutching the bell-
push tight in the other, until at last the door opened. Phyllis
stood there, swaying slightly, her hair, ashen-coloured, falling on to her shoulders. Her dressing-gown was a white
quilted one, with little pink flowers in sprigs all over it,
ridiculous, more suitable for Cathy.

"What is it, Mother?" said Phyllis, coming towards her and
blinking in the sudden light. "Can't you sleep? Haven't you
taken your pill?"

Mrs. Ludlow stared at her. What did she want, coming in
like this, a caricature of the child she had been? She forgot
that she had summoned her. She allowed the bell to be taken
from her grasp and her pillows plumped up while she thought.

There was that policeman, the one who had sat in Gerald's
swivel chair. There was something he must not know, or it
would cause trouble. What was it?

Ah! The visitors on Saturday, that was it; her secret. First
Derek, then Tim, and later Martin. Stupid boys, all of them,
thinking she would save them from their own folly. They
must learn that money did not grow on trees. Well, the

police could only hear of their visits through her, and she had not told, nor would she. They would not give themselves away.

Tim had not told his grandmother that he had already seen Phyllis, and the idea that he might have done so did not occur to her.

"I want a drink," she said, and "How clumsy you are," as Phyllis emptied her glass of water and filled it afresh. In spite of the waves of sleep which kept surging over her, Phyllis had not spilled a drop, nor made any noise.

"Now read to me," said Mrs. Ludlow.

Phyllis opened her eyes very wide; weights seemed to press down their lids.

"I've forgotten my glasses," she said, and when her scolding was over she was allowed to go back to her room for them. Once there, she washed her face in cold water, splashing it into her eyes and round the back of her neck.

Her mother seemed to be dozing again when she returned, but her eyes opened as soon as Phyllis crossed the threshold. She was not released until nearly four o'clock. Each time that Phyllis thought her mother had fallen asleep, and stopped reading, Mrs. Ludlow snapped: "Go on, go on, I'm not asleep," though her eyes were closed. It was will-power alone that kept her awake, thought Phyllis.

The sky was light and the birds were starting their morning twitter by the time she got back to her own bed.

THURSDAY

I

"What an hour to face your mentor," Jane said. "Why didn't you deal with him last night?"

Timothy had been to Reynard's, received a mammoth sermon followed by some constructive help, and had departed, chastened but relieved. Now Jane, who had not been allowed to offer the boy even a cup of coffee, sat facing her brother across the kitchen table. Patrick was busy polishing off a large helping of eggs, bacon and tomatoes. The pleasant atmosphere in the kitchen, with its checked gingham curtains, red-topped table, and pine dresser hung with Cornish ware, had a softening effect on him, so that he began to wonder if his stately bachelor apartments in St. Mark's were quite so enviable after all.

"There was far too much of more importance going on," he said. "Besides, it was good for him to have another night on the rack, and have to get up early. I got there last night just in time to stop him from making a clean breast of everything, thus unloading his own guilt but helping no one else."

Jane handed a sliver of toast to young Andrew, who was seated in his high chair waving a spoon in one fist.

"I don't like you casting yourself in the role of God," she said. "Who are you to think that you know best?"

"My dear girl, that young wretch is my responsibility, whatever I may think about it. I'm quite certain his misdeeds have no connection with this larger problem, but if the police heard about them, they might have to pay official heed. Mind you, it might be better for the boy in the long run to face the consequences, be up before the beak and so forth. But his parents have enough on their plates without him adding to it."

"Borrowing a car that wasn't insured without its owner's permission, and then piling it up. Is it such a terrible crime?" Jane asked.

"It could be called theft," said Patrick. "True, the car belonged to a so-called friend, and true that young Tim didn't know it wasn't insured, but he took it while its owner was away, and then he piled it up. Suppose someone had been hurt? Then he would have been in quite a lot of trouble. As it is, there's simply a hefty repair bill to be met."

"Hm." Jane was not convinced. "I believe it's a crime to withhold information from the police," she said.

"Information related to a crime," said Patrick. "This boy has merely been grossly irresponsible, and that's a fair description of his university life thus far. But he isn't a hopeless case. There's no bad core in him. His mother has doted on him to excess, and his father has been disinterested. Add to that the pressures of the day and a weak character, and you have young Ludlow. The other boy is weak too; no doubt that's what drew him to this flighty girl he married. But he's much more likeable than Timothy. Of course, he's four years older."

"But why should they be like that? Their parents seem all right. Solid citizens, in spite of the business disaster. It isn't Derek Ludlow who's pinched the client's money, after all."

"No, but he wasn't vigilant enough to spot what was happening under his nose. I think indifference is the culprit," Patrick said. "Good old *laissez-faire*."

"Well, that's something you can't be accused of," Jane said caustically. "I wish you'd *laisse* a little more to *faire* for itself."

"Indifference is one of the sins of the age," Patrick said. "Passing by on the other side. But you worry too much, sister dear. As it is, the police will take ages to sort all this out. They have to check so much. Their work is like a scholar's research, a mass of detail to be sifted very patiently. Foster may have to fly someone out to Canada, or have the relevant documents sent over here. That takes time, and meanwhile something else may turn up. There must be proof, if only I can find it."

"You think you know what happened?"

"I'm sure of it. It all clicks, but I can't prove anything, and my theories won't convince the Inspector without some facts to back them up."

"It's horrible," Jane said. "You could be wrong."

"It's still horrible, even if I am," said Patrick. He helped himself to a slice of toast and some marmalade.

"I hope the other boy, Martin, will be all right," said Jane.

"He will," said Patrick cheerfully. "He's well rid of that gold-digger."

"He sounds a sensitive type, from what you say. It may have gone very deep," Jane said.

"I'll send him round to visit you," Patrick promised. "Tea and sympathy from an older woman are what he needs to fix him."

"What a cynic you are," said Jane. "I hope no girl's ever fool enough to marry you." She wiped a dab of honey from her son's snub nose. "Don't take after your uncle, poppet," she advised. "Nosey, vain and interfering, that's what he is, and heartless to boot." She poured the remaining coffee into her own cup. "You don't deserve any more," she said to Patrick. "You can wait till I brew another pot."

Patrick got up and went to the back door. Outside, the garden wore wreaths of dewy cobwebs on the hedges and the flowers. The air felt fresh, and the sun was up; it would be another lovely day. Heartless, was he? He felt in his pocket for his pipe, took it out, and lit it. It wasn't true. He felt deeply stirred with pity for some of the people involved in this unhappy drama, but infuriated with the folly of others. Unheeding stupidity was to him a wicked thing, deserving of no sympathy, and sentiment must not be allowed to cloud judgement.

He walked slowly down the garden, meditating, puffing at his pipe. A clump of love-in-a-mist, blue, blooming late, caught his eye. The colour, though a paler shade, was that of the capsules Mrs. Mackenzie had been given. They had been opened, the powder taken out, the empty capsules thrown away, or swallowed boldly, perhaps. Absently he picked a flower head, twirled it between his fingers, and walked towards the gate. His car was parked outside, in the lane, where he had left it the night before. He crossed over to it, laid the flower on the bonnet, took a leather from the glove compartment and began to clean the windscreen.

II

"I'm all right, darling, really. Please stop worrying," said Helen. She sat up in bed, her shoulders very white against the soft peach colour of her nightdress. Her eyes looked huge in the pallor of her face.

"Well, don't get up yet," Gerald said. He sat on the side of the bed holding her hand and looking at her anxiously. "I must ring up the office, and then I must talk to Derek. He seems to be in a hell of a mess, one way and another. I'll come back when I'm through with all that and see how you are. You snuggle down till then."

"That Bludgen witch will be here today. Send her home, Gerry," Helen said. "I can't face her."

"You needn't. She can stay downstairs."

"Oh Gerry, no! Please send her home, or up to Phyllis. She could use her, surely? She gives me the creeps," said Helen. "Imagine her working here all those years and then spying on you all and telling the police about everyone's movements."

"To be fair to the Bludgen, she can't have had any idea of what's at stake," said Gerald. "In any case, as a law-abiding citizen she's obliged to answer the questions of the police."

"I suppose so. All the same, I don't like her," Helen said.

"Well, darling, if you really feel so strongly, of course I'll send her home," said Gerald. He bent to kiss her. "Just you rest. There's nothing to worry about," he added, and went out of the room.

But when the door was closed behind him his face lost its calm expression. There was a very great deal to worry about, but he could think of nothing to be done to improve the situation.

He went heavily down the stairs.

Clattering sounds came from the kitchen, where Mrs. Bludgen was already at work washing up the glasses from the night before. When Gerald told her that she could go home as soon as this task was completed she looked surprised, but did not protest. She accepted the two pounds he gave her and put them in the pocket of her flowered pinafore; then she polished the glasses with tremendous application, put them away, and left. He watched her walk down the path with her quick, bouncing step, her brilliant curls glittering in the sunlight. How well-disposed in fact was she? If she really was ignorant of what was at the bottom of the police inquiries, she was probably harmless, but if she understood she might take it into her head to telephone Fleet Street. He thought about pursuing her with pleas for discretion, but dismissed the idea. She would do it anyway, if she thought of it. She was the type who couldn't resist sensation.

He went back into the house and telephoned his office. Once that task was done he could think about matters nearer at hand. His conversation lasted for over half an hour. Then he spoke to Derek. Phyllis, last night, had supplied more details of his disastrous predicament, when everyone else had gone home. A very depressed voice answered him. They had a guarded conversation, for it would not do to be overheard, and agreed to meet in the evening.

"How are things with you?" Derek asked.

"Nothing new," Gerald said.

"How's Helen this morning?" In spite of his own misfortunes Derek had time to spare sympathy for his brother's plight.

"Oh, still a bit upset," Gerald said.

Derek was surprised that she seemed to be at home; he thought she must at least be "helping the police with their inquiries."

"It's the lull before the storm, I think," Gerald said. "It can't last."

"No. How's Mother?"

"Seems to be all right. Phyl is being pretty good. Cathy will have to be told what happened last night."

"I suppose so. God, what a mess," said Derek. "Well, I must go. I've got to see my lawyers. We'll talk tonight."

"Right. Good luck," Gerald said.

"And you."

The brothers rang off, feeling warmer towards one another than they had done for years. Gerald sat by the telephone for some minutes, thinking. Could anything be done? Should he get on to the lawyers too? How would the police react to last night's disclosure? The shocked faces of his own family were a portent. Helen was in grave peril.

He must go up to her, but there was nothing consoling to say; it was only a question of time before the police arrived.

He stood up, but before he had reached the foot of the stairs
Cathy came into the house.

"How's Helen?" she asked. "Aunt Phyl said she didn't feel
well last night. I came to see if I could do anything."

"She's still a bit peaky," Gerald said. "Come up and see
her," Cathy would be a diversion, and mean postponing a
discussion on what could be done, to which there was no
answer.

"The police were here for ages last night," Cathy said.

"Yes. They dug up all the family skeletons," said Gerald.

"Aunt Phyl said Dr. Grant was here. I like him. He wants
to help us," Cathy said.

"He seems to have got young Tim taped," said Gerald.
Beyond this he could think of nothing good to say about the
Dean of St. Mark's.

By this time they had reached the landing. Gerald tapped
on the bedroom door and opened it.

The room was empty.

The bed was made, but there was no sign of Helen.

Gerald, alarm in his voice, called her, but there was no
answer. He pushed past Cathy and opened the bathroom
door, but she was not there. Then he hunted all over the
house, but she was nowhere to be found. It was Cathy who
saw that her little overnight bag had disappeared with her
brushes and make-up from the dressing-table, and who found
the note left in their place.

"Oh, Daddy, she's gone!" Cathy cried.

Gerald tore open the envelope with feverish fingers and
took out the sheet of paper that was in it.

My darling Gerald, he read, in Helen's neat, small
handwriting.

> *When you find this note you will know that I have gone.
> Please don't raise the alarm; that way I shall have a chance
> to get ahead of your police before they come for me. I know
> they must do this when they find out how I met Joyce
> Mackenzie, for they will realise I would not want your
> family to learn about it.*
>
> *It was asking too much to hope for another chance.
> Whoever loads the dice must have laughed at my coming to
> the one house in England where I would be recognised.*
>
> *Bless you, dearest Gerry, and forgive me.*
>
> > *Helen.*

Gerald read this through twice. Then he folded it up again and put it in his pocket.

"What's happened, Daddy? Couldn't she bear all this police business?" Cathy asked.

"That's it, more or less," said Gerald.

Cathy was frightened, looking at her father. His face was grey and there were queer lines round his mouth that she had never seen before.

"Oh Daddy! But she'll come back when it's all over," she tried to reassure him. "We'll get her back. Where has she gone?"

"I don't know." Gerald thumped his head with his clenched fists. "Oh God, what am I to do?" he groaned.

Timidly Cathy put her hand on his arm.

"We could go after her," she said. "When do you think she went?"

"She must have slipped out while I was on the telephone," said Gerald. That was why she had wanted Mrs. Bludgen sent away. "I've been talking for over an hour."

"She hasn't taken the car," Cathy said. "It was in the garage just now as I came in."

"She can't have got far, then," Gerald said. What could be in Helen's mind? Where would she plan to go, in a strange country, without much money—for he knew she could not have very much in her purse. How could she hope to elude the police? They would catch up with her all right, and by running away she had made things look so black for herself. Her best hope, when the police came to question her, would have been to face up to them, but what a thing to expect of her after her former experiences.

Mrs. Bludgen would have seen her leave. Helen would not have known how to cross the meadow and get over the fence, avoiding the lodge. But Gerald would not waste time asking her.

"You're right, I'll go after her," he said. "She'll be aiming for the station." He strode out to the garage, followed by Cathy.

"I'm coming too," she said.

"London's the only place she knows. That's where she'll go," Gerald said, getting into the car.

"My bike's gone," Cathy said. "Look! She's taken it."

"Christ!" said Gerald. He shoved the car into gear and backed rapidly out of the garage, catching a geranium tub as he turned. They drove off down the drive, Cathy sitting forward as if she might see Helen pedalling in front of them.

"If she's biking to the station it will take her ages," said Cathy. "She's got that little suitcase with her, that vanity one. It will slow her up. We'll catch her, Daddy."

"I hope you're right," said Gerald. He caught a glimpse of Mrs. Bludgen's face, a round white disc pressed to the window as they passed the lodge. Wretched woman.

Cathy's eyes were fixed on the way ahead. An agony was in her heart. If Helen really loved her father she would not run away when things were bad for him.

"She won't know the way," Gerald said, between gritted teeth. She would be in danger, too, cycling along on what was to her the wrong side of the road. How did she expect to manage it?

They passed Reynard's. Patrick's car was parked outside the cottage in the lane. There was no time to notice if Andrew's pram was under the apple tree. Then they drove into Winterswick, forced to slacken their speed at the road junction.

"There's my bike, look, by the bus shelter!" Cathy cried.

"Sure it's yours?"

"Yes, I think so. Slow up."

Cathy jumped out, ran to the bike and looked at it, and then jumped back into the car.

"It's mine all right," she said. Her name was neatly painted on the mudguard, a requirement of her school so lately left. "There's a bus to Fennersham at a quarter to ten, she must have caught it."

Gerald put his foot down hard and the big car surged forward. Nevertheless the journey into the town was fraught with hazard; a laundry van rushed out in front of them from a side turning, they met three cows being driven down the road, and the traffic lights at the foot of the High Street turned red as they approached, but at last they reached the station, only to find that the London train had left half an hour before.

"We could have worked that out for ourselves. It would have been better to drive straight to Waterloo and hope to catch her there," said Gerald bitterly.

"You'd never have done it, Daddy," Cathy said gently. She thought her heart would break for him, he was so stricken. He sat in the car with his shoulders sagging, looking old.

"Derek might go. He might find her," Gerald said suddenly, sitting up. "I'll ring him."

It was something, anyway; a chance. At least the thought of it removed that hopeless look from his face. He drove into the yard of the Lamb Hotel near the station and asked to use the telephone.

Cathy sat waiting in the car. It was so terribly sad. She felt wretched on her own account, too, for she had liked Helen and thought they would get on well together once they had learned to know one another just a little better.

Gerald came back some ten minutes later. He seemed calmer, but his face was still grey. He got into the car beside Cathy and sat for a moment gripping the steering-wheel.

"Uncle Derek wasn't in his office," he said. Derek had gone round to his solicitor's. There was no point in trying to ring him there, he would either have left, or be too distracted on his own account. Gerald had rung up Martin, who was in such deep trouble anyway not only with his private cares, but also with his office for his ill-justified absences, that he thought another defection more or less would make no odds. He agreed to waylay Helen and try to persuade her to go home with him to the Chelsea house; Gerald could then come and fetch her, or, if she would not return, stay up there too.

He told Cathy this.

"We'll go home," he said. "Martin will ring as soon as he can, so I must be there."

They drove silently back to the Stable House, stopping in Winterswick to pick up Cathy's bicycle which was still in its resting-place by the bus shelter. It had been transported in the boot of Gerald's car often enough before. By the time they reached the house Gerald had made up his mind to tell Cathy the full story of what had happened the night before so that she should understand why Helen had fled.

Trying to speak very calmly, he told her. Cathy did not interrupt, but her eyes grew larger and larger as she listened, and once or twice she gasped.

"Poor Helen," she said at the end. "Oh, Daddy, how awful!" She got up from the sofa where she had been sitting and perched on the arm of his chair, where she rubbed her cheek against his as she had done when she was a little girl. "She must love you very much." She was so relieved that her father had not, after all, been emotionally cheated that at first this was her only thought. But soon she felt a wider reaction.

"But it's mad to think like that," she said. "How could the police believe such a thing? Of course she didn't do it."

"Who did, then?" Gerald asked.

Cathy stared at him.

"You don't mean you believe she did?" she said, appalled.

"No, of course not, chicken," said Gerald. "But it puts us back into square one with the original idea of someone trying to kill your grandmother."

"I'd rather believe that than this other thing," Cathy said, shuddering. "Oh Daddy, it's like some dreadful nightmare!"

"It is." And it was dreadful for his young daughter to be so deeply involved. The two people in the world most precious to Gerald were in it up to the hilt, but of them both there was no doubt that Cathy was the tougher; less had been demanded of her, thus far in her life, in the way of courage and resilience. He could not tell her what it was he feared so gravely now. When Martin telephoned to say that Helen had not been on the train that arrived at Waterloo from Fennersham he admitted, but only to himself, his utter terror.

III

Soon after twelve o'clock Inspector Foster arrived at the Stable House with a warrant for Helen's arrest. With a set face Gerald said that she had gone away and he had no idea where she might be. Beyond that, he said nothing. The house was searched by Sergeant Smithers, who looked extremely uncomfortable, and a policewoman who had come too. After this the Inspector took his little troop away; they went straight down the drive towards the lodge.

"Mrs. Bludgen will soon tell him what time Helen left," Gerald thought. He felt it vital to stay near the telephone: how else could Helen find him if she wanted him? Cathy had gone back to Pantons to help her aunt and to tell her what had happened, but Gerald thought that they should keep as quiet as possible about Helen's disappearance. Derek would tell Betty that night, if the police had not found her by then.

Phyllis was in the kitchen making a sauce. Cathy peeled potatoes while they talked. Grandmother's appetite remained unaffected by what went on beyond her room.

"She's asked for Helen several times this morning," Phyllis

said. "She seems to have taken a fancy to her. Helen promised to read to her today."

"What did you say?"

"Well, I rang the Stable House and couldn't get an answer, so I said the phone was out of order," Phyllis said. "Now that you've told me about it, I'll say Helen's got a headache."

"Isn't it awful, Aunt Phyl? Helen's had such a terrible time already. It isn't fair."

"It isn't," Phyllis agreed. But life seldom was. "I suppose Gerald never mentioned Mrs. Mackenzie's name when he was telling her about the set-up here. There must have been hundreds of women in that prison, too. It had to be one she'd known quite well." She poured the sauce over some flaked cod in a fireproof dish. "She said they were quite friendly."

"Poor Daddy's very unhappy," Cathy said.

"Of course he is," said Phyllis.

"I think he's afraid that Helen might—well, she wasn't on that train," said Cathy. She dared not put into words the thing that had crossed her mind.

"Trains go in two directions," Phyllis said. "Helen may have gone the other way."

"I hadn't thought of that." Cathy looked more hopeful. "I was afraid Dad thought she might—"

"I doubt it," Phyllis said. "Helen's been through a lot already. If she was the type to commit suicide she'd have done it years ago." Brisk words, and empty ones, for who could tell what might make a person snap? Helen was the sort of person to do what she thought would cause those she loved the least distress. A quiet disappearance into a river, perhaps, to be found in a few days' time, would tie up neatly the mystery of Joyce Mackenzie's death without too much damaging reflection on the Ludlows. Phyllis ran water into the saucepan she had used and scrubbed it fiercely with the scourer.

A pealing sound made both her and Cathy jump. It was Mrs. Ludlow's bell.

"I'll go," said Cathy. "It's my turn." She dried her hands and left the kitchen. She seemed to her aunt to have grown up almost overnight; she was proving to be a tower of strength.

Cathy found her grandmother playing patience on a table that she could swing across her chair.

"Well, Gran, what is it?" she asked briskly.

"Oh, it's you. I want Helen," Mrs. Ludlow said. "She promised to read to me today. I like her voice."

"I'll read to you, Gran," said Cathy. "Which book is it?"

"No, no. Helen promised. I want her," said Mrs. Ludlow pettishly.

"She can't come. She's got a headache," Cathy said. "Is this the one?" She picked up a book that was on the table at her grandmother's side.

"Tch, tch, child." Mrs. Ludlow waved her off. "Take these away," she said, and pushed at the hinged table, sending the cards flying.

Cathy started to pick them up, and heard her grandmother lift the telephone.

"Gerald, Gerald, is that you?" came her voice.

Poor Daddy. He would expect the call to be something to do with Helen.

"Where's Helen? She promised to read to me today," said Mrs. Ludlow.

Cathy could hear the murmur of her father's voice.

"I want to speak to her," Mrs. Ludlow said.

More mumblings from Gerald.

"Well, it's too bad of her," said Mrs. Ludlow crossly. "I'm annoyed," and she rang off.

"Gone to the village indeed," she grumbled. "She hasn't got a headache." She moved in her chair, reaching for her stick, and held it between her hands, rubbing the silver top. "Very well, Cathy. You shall read instead."

Cathy picked up the book, took out the marker from the page where Phyllis had left it in the early hours after her vigil, and began. Mrs. Ludlow seemed to listen, but every now and then she muttered to herself under her breath and caused Cathy to falter in her stride. She made Cathy read till lunch was ready, and then ate every morsel on her plate while Phyllis and Cathy pushed tiny portions of fish and vegetables around with their forks and hardly swallowed a mouthful.

Afterwards, Mrs. Ludlow refused to go upstairs for her daily rest, an interval that meant respite for the whole house as well as for her.

"I'm not resting today," she said. "Helen will be coming. She didn't this morning, so she'll come this afternoon. Wheel me back to the drawing-room."

She banged her stick on the floor to emphasise her words. Phyllis and Cathy exchanged glances.

"Please, Mother. You'll be tired if you don't rest," said Phyllis.

"I rest all day," snapped Mrs. Ludlow. "Do as I say."

Cathy wheeled her back to her corner in the drawing-room, put a glass of water where she could reach it and marched out of the room. Gran was worse than a naughty child. She went to help her aunt clear away, and as they loaded the trolley they both heard the tell-tale click that meant the telephone was being used.

Shamelessly they went into the hall and stood there listening.

"Gerald? Gerald? I want to speak to Helen," they heard.

There was a pause and then the old, deep voice came again.

"There's something wrong. Don't lie to me. Is she ill?"

There was another silence, then some muttering. Finally Mrs. Ludlow's bell pealed vigorously.

"Never mind the plates. Let's both go," Phyllis said.

Side by side, aunt and niece entered the drawing-room. Mrs. Ludlow sat in her chair with her eyes glittering.

"Now then, you two. Wheel me down to the Stable House, at once," she said. "I don't care which of you does it. There's something wrong, and I'm going to see for myself what it is."

"No, Mother. You stay here," said Phyllis in a soothing voice. "Helen's just upset after the journey. She'll come up and see you when she's better."

"Wheel me down, I said," Mrs. Ludlow repeated. "Cathy, you do it, since your aunt seems determined to defy her own mother."

"I'll take you down to the Stable House, if you wish, Mrs. Ludlow," said a new voice, and to the astonishment of everyone Patrick appeared through the french window. "I happened to overhear," he said.

Cathy had always before been pleased to see him, but not this time. She frowned at him, but he avoided her eye, bending over her grandmother so that she did not have to peer up to look at him.

"Thank you indeed, Dr. Grant," she said, with a gracious nod of her head. She picked up her stick and laid it across her knees, over the rug that always covered them. "You'll find the chair propels quite easily," she informed him.

Patrick bowed to the other two and pushed the old lady past them, out of the room, without another word.

Phyllis and Cathy were too surprised to move for a moment, but then Phyllis seized the telephone.

"We must warn your father," she said, dialling the number.

Patrick, meanwhile, made no haste. He chatted about the weather, admired the plants they passed, and commented on the current political situation as he picked out the smoothest course for the chair. When they arrived at the Stable House Gerald had had time to adopt a mask of calm. He left the front door open so that Patrick could wheel his mother in without difficulty, then prepared to feign surprise; it was useless to try to stop her once she had made up her mind to take any action, but that fellow from Oxford seemed to have an extraordinary aptitude for throwing spanners into the works.

He heard the sound of the chair crossing the cobbles, and then Patrick's voice, cheerfully raised.

"Is anyone at home?" he called. "I've brought a visitor."

"Wheel me in, wheel me in," commanded Mrs. Ludlow with impatience. She clasped her stick upright as they passed between the doorposts, balancing it between her feet on the foot-rest of her chair.

"Mother! What a nice surprise! And Dr. Grant too! Come in," cried Gerald valiantly.

Full marks, thought Patrick, pushing on.

"I've come to see what's wrong with Helen," said Mrs. Ludlow, going straight to the point. "Phyllis said she'd a headache, and you say she went to the village. What's the truth of it?"

"Well, she did have a headache, and she thought a walk might clear it away, so she went to the village. But she still isn't well, so she's resting," Gerald said.

His mother fixed him with a beady stare.

"Don't lie to me, Gerald," she said. "I want the truth."

"She's sleeping, Mother. I'm not going to wake her," said Gerald. He looked steadily back at his mother.

"I can always tell when you're lying, Gerald," said Mrs. Ludlow. "Don't waste my time. What's happened?"

Gerald turned his back to her and put a hand to his head.

"I'm waiting, Gerald," said Mrs. Ludlow. He might have been ten years old. He swung round to face her again.

"Very well. You'll have to find out, I suppose, sooner or later. She's left me," he said.

There was absolute silence. Then, in a voice from which all vibrancy had gone, Mrs. Ludlow said: "But why?"

"She was upset by Mrs. Mackenzie's death," answered Gerald shortly. He turned his back to her again and kicked at the fender.

"Stop fidgeting, Gerald, and look at me," said Mrs. Ludlow, more firmly. "Why should she be upset? There was nothing to fear."

"Mrs. Ludlow, I think your family has been trying to hide from you the fact that the police are not satisfied about the manner in which Mrs. Mackenzie died," said Patrick in a quiet voice.

"Oh, damn you, Grant; haven't you done enough damage? Get out of here," stormed Gerald, rounding on him.

"Don't go, Dr. Grant," said Mrs. Ludlow sharply. "You'll tell me the truth. Why are the police not satisfied?"

"She had a dubious past, it seems," said Patrick in a mild voice. "They think she was poisoned because of it."

"Is this true? Gerald, what have they found out?" Mrs. Ludlow's voice was a hiss.

"Mrs. Mackenzie has been in prison, Mother. You knew that, didn't you?"

"Yes, of course I did. You know I did," said Mrs. Ludlow.

"The police think that Mrs. Mackenzie knew something discreditable about Helen Ludlow as a result of her prison sentence," said Patrick. He waited. "They think that Helen Ludlow may have murdered Mrs. Mackenzie," he said.

There was a sudden clatter. Mrs. Ludlow's stick fell from her knees and rolled forward across the polished floor. Patrick instinctively moved to pick it up, then checked; the old lady had propelled her chair forward herself and was reaching down for it, but Gerald forestalled her. He gave it to her silently. She laid it across her knees again and Patrick saw the old, gnarled fingers twitching at her rug.

"Helen didn't poison her," said Mrs. Ludlow.

"Of course she didn't," Gerald said. "But the police won't believe it."

"It was meant for me," said Mrs. Ludlow. Her voice shook. "The police believed that, didn't they? Joyce Mackenzie took it by mistake. It was her greed that killed her."

There was silence in the room. Patrick did not move, but his eyes flicked from the old woman's face to Gerald's, waiting to see if he registered what he had heard. Very, very slowly, Gerald realised its significance.

"You knew about it," he said. "No one told you about the tablets, but you knew!"

"Of course I knew," said Mrs. Ludlow roughly. "All those policemen about the place, asking questions. I'm not in my second childhood yet, you know."

"But you couldn't have known, mother," said Gerald. He gazed at her in horror. "How could you know?"

"I guessed, of course. Anyone with any brains would do the same," Mrs. Ludlow blustered, but Gerald simply stood there gaping at her.

"Mrs. Ludlow, the police will arrest Helen Ludlow and charge her with the murder, as soon as she is found," said Patrick. "That is why she's gone away."

Gerald's head jerked, and he glared at Patrick, but Patrick paid him no attention.

"You knew that Mrs. Mackenzie was already dead on Sunday morning, when you rang your bell, didn't you?" he said. "That was why you told Mrs. Medhurst to go and call her, not your granddaughter. You tried to stop Cathy from finding her. How did you know that Mrs. Mackenzie was dead, Mrs. Ludlow?"

She stared at him, this friend turned sudden foe.

"It will all be for nothing, won't it, Mrs. Ludlow, if Helen is arrested?" said Patrick softly. "Hadn't you better tell us what you did?"

There was no reply. A little gasping sound came from the old lady, that was all. Patrick went on talking.

"You knew that if you didn't eat your pudding, Mrs. Mackenzie would be sure to finish it," he said. "It was easy for you to open some of your pills and slip the powder into the meringue, wasn't it? You had plenty of time to do it."

"But—why?" whispered Gerald. "Why?"

"Because your mother loves you, Mr. Ludlow," Patrick said in a gentle voice. "That's right, isn't it, Mrs. Ludlow?"

She did not speak, but she grunted and gave a feeble nod. She had sunk down in her chair, and her once proud head dropped forward on to her bony chest, the eyes downcast.

"When Mrs. Mackenzie and your wife recognised each other on Friday night, you decided the best course was to tell your mother the truth, hoping the rest of the family need never know. That's right, isn't it?" Patrick said to Gerald.

The other man nodded, his eyes still on his mother in horrified fascination.

"Of all her children, you are the only one that Mrs. Ludlow has real feeling for," said Patrick. "She wanted your happiness. It's the normal wish of any mother. Mrs. Ludlow thought that it would be threatened if your secret was discovered. She told you to keep away while she spoke to Mrs. Mackenzie and made her promise not to tell. That is why you went to London on Saturday. Correct?"

Gerald nodded again.

"But you didn't trust Mrs. Mackenzie, did you, Mrs. Ludlow? You thought you'd better make quite sure," said Patrick.

"Mother, is this true?" Gerald spoke at last.

A little croak was all they heard in answer.

"Mother, you must tell the police what you've done," said Gerald. "They think Helen did it. Mother, don't you understand? You must tell them, Mother!"

But Mrs. Ludlow could not tell anybody anything. She made a gurgling noise and slumped forward in her chair. Patrick caught her just before she fell.

IV

They lifted the old lady gently out of her chair and laid her on the sofa. She was pitifully light. Gerald picked up her rug from where it had fallen and draped it over her. Deep, rasping breaths came from her, and her mouth gaped.

"I'll ring the doctor," Gerald said.

"Call the police too," said Patrick. He feared that Helen's picture might be splashed on the front page of all the evening papers, under banner headlines. He had picked up Mrs. Ludlow's silver-headed stick and was examining it curiously. The handle was chased, and bore some initials on it in a monogram.

"I suppose I must," said Gerald. He looked at Patrick with a desolate expression; all his anger had vanished. "This lets Helen out. But where is she? It may be too late."

Gerald put Mrs. Ludlow's stick carefully down on her wheel-chair. He laid a hand on Gerald's arm.

"She's safe," he said. "Brace up, man. She's with my sister.

I'm sorry I couldn't let you know earlier, but you'd never have played up if you'd known she was all right."

Gerald was astounded. His immediate reaction was of immense relief, but soon it was replaced by incredulity.

"You mean you planned all this?" he asked, making a gesture that embraced the whole room, including the helpless figure of his mother.

"Not in quite this fashion, and certainly without such an ending," Patrick said. He glanced at the inert form. Perhaps it was for the best. "I knew your mother had killed Mrs. Mackenzie. I came up to see if I could find some proof." In fact he had slipped into Pantons by the back door while Mrs. Ludlow, Phyllis and Cathy were at lunch. He had travelled up in the lift and poked about in Mrs. Ludlow's room, but without finding what he sought. "I heard your mother insist on coming down here, and I thought she might trap herself."

"I can't take it in," Gerald said, shaking his head. "How did you know?"

"She tried to prevent Cathy from waking Mrs. Mackenzie. That wasn't a natural reaction. She wanted to save her from shock, because her affection for you included your daughter. Cathy told me in detail what happened on Sunday morning; she said her aunt told her to go to Mrs. Mackenzie's room, and Mrs. Ludlow said: 'Don't send the child, you go, Phyllis.' Cathy was quite definite about it, because it made her indignant on her aunt's behalf."

"Will the police believe it?"

"I think so," Patrick said. "Unless I'm much mistaken, we shall find our proof. Will you ring them, or shall I?"

"I will," said Gerald. He straightened himself, cast one more look at his mother, and then went to the telephone.

When he had made the two calls he lit a cigarette, and Patrick took out his pipe. They sat together, smoking silently.

"I suppose there's nothing we can do for Mother?" Gerald said at last. "The doctor won't be long."

"She's past our help, I'm afraid," said Patrick. "The shock must have been too much for her."

"She never gave a sign, these past days. Her appetite, even! It never faltered."

"Iron self-control," said Patrick. "Our generation hasn't got it to the same extent. She was sure that she could win."

"But how did Helen get to your sister's? Did she go straight to you this morning? I've been nearly frantic," Gerald said. "I was afraid she might do something desperate," he confessed. "Silly, I suppose."

"Not at all. She was in a bad way this morning, and I'm not surprised," said Patrick. "She's been under a dreadful strain, and so have you. I happened to see her riding by on her bicycle. Or rather, Cathy's bicycle. I hope it didn't get pinched, by the way. I left it by the bus stop as a decoy."

"It's all right. I rescued it," said Gerald.

"Good. Well, as I say, I happened to see your wife pedalling along when I was cleaning my car." He paused. "She's not a very skilful cyclist, I'm afraid. She did a nasty swerve and skidded off." No wonder, at his ambush. He had almost given her up, when she appeared. "She didn't hurt herself," he said. He thought of Helen, sobbing in Jane's kitchen, hysterical at last. But she had calmed down in the end, and listened to him. Then she consented to be hidden for the day, and to trust him.

"I seem to be rather heavily in your debt," said Gerald gruffly. "And your sister's, too."

Patrick waved a deprecating hand.

"We're not quite out of the wood yet," he said. "There's a car now. Doctor, or police?"

It was Inspector Foster. He came striding in, with Sergeant Smithers in his wake, and halted at the sight of Mrs. Ludlow lying on the sofa, still breathing stertorously.

"We need an ambulance," he said. "Sergeant!"

"Dr. Wilkins is on his way," said Gerald. "Please don't take my mother from her home."

"Well, now, what is all this?" demanded the Inspector. "I'm sorry Mrs. Ludlow's ill, of course. But you said on the telephone that fresh evidence had come to light."

Patrick stepped foward, and the Inspector looked at him in a weary way as if to say: "What, you again?"

"Before she was taken ill Mrs. Ludlow admitted putting barbiturate powder in the helping of lemon meringue pie on her tray," he said. "She dropped her stick when she fell. I picked it up, but otherwise I have not touched it. If you unscrew the silver top you may find something interesting inside."

The Inspector looked at him, then at the stick, lying so innocently across the arms of the empty wheel-chair. He lifted it, holding it gingerly with a handkerchief around his

own fingers, and gave the top a twist. It unscrewed and he
tipped it up. Into the palm of his hand fell several empty
blue gelatine containers, and five whole sodium amytal
capsules.

V

At Reynard's the curtains were drawn, and Jane had lit a fire
of apple logs in the open hearth. Round it sat a subdued little
group: Phyllis, Gerald, with Helen at his side, and Cathy,
and beyond them, Patrick and Jane.

"How's Mrs. Ludlow now?" asked Jane. She bent to poke
the fire, and a splutter of flames crackled. A rich fragrance
came from the old wood as it burned.

"Not too good," said Phyllis.

No one else spoke. All knew it was for the best, but they
could not say so. Mrs. Ludlow had been taken back to her
own bed, and a nurse had arrived. Outside the door of her
room sat the same policewoman who had come to the Stable
House only that morning to arrest Helen.

"I just can't believe it," Cathy said at last. "For Gran to
think up such a thing—it was mad!"

"She was power-mad, Cathy," said Patrick. To him, one of
the strangest features of the case was the way in which Mrs.
Ludlow had cold-bloodedly accepted that some of her family
might wish for her death. "For years she had controlled you
all—or she thought so. She could cut off funds at source, or
deprive you of your expectations. When the happiness of her
favourite child was threatened by a fantastic coincidence, she
would not let things rest. She took upon herself the mantle of
fate."

"I wanted to talk to Joyce," Helen said, in her soft voice.
"After all, it was her secret too. But Mrs. Ludlow said Sunday would be soon enough."

"Poor Gran. She must have been all mixed up," said Cathy.
"I suppose, when you've been ill for years—" her voice
trailed off. Invalids did not always develop megalomania.
"She could be nice. We had our laughs," she said. But they
were very few; Gran had been cruel, especially to Aunt Phyl.
She realised that already she was speaking of her grandmother in the past tense, and shivered.

"I don't understand how you discovered what happened, Dr. Grant," said Phyllis.

"Something in Cathy's description of what happened on Sunday morning kept nagging at me," Patrick said. "I didn't at first realise its significance. You asked Cathy to wake Mrs. Mackenzie, and Mrs. Ludlow tried to prevent her from going. She wanted to spare her from a terrible experience. And on Saturday afternoon, your grandmother sent you to the vicarage with a letter, didn't she, Cathy?

"I think there were two reasons for this errand. The first was to get you, Cathy, out of the house because she wanted time to fetch the capsules from the hall without fear of interruption."

"If only I'd put them away," said Phyllis.

"She would have got them even more easily, for they would have been in her room. It wouldn't have made any difference," Patrick said. It would have made Phyllis prime suspect of the supposed attempt to kill Mrs. Ludlow; otherwise Mrs. Ludlow's plans would not have been affected.

"But mother couldn't have fetched the pills from the hall," said Gerald. "She couldn't move."

"She could. I wasn't sure about this," said Patrick. "But this afternoon, don't you remember, she dropped her stick and she moved her chair forward to reach it. If she had plenty of time, she could have done it."

"I've seen her move," Phyllis said. "She used to get about quite well on her own, but her arms have got very weak now."

"And also she wanted you to push her about," said Patrick. "Remember that. She wanted you at her beck and call. She probably propelled herself about quite often, if no one was there to see. Anyway, with Cathy out at the vicarage, would she have known when you or Mrs. Mackenzie were likely to interrupt her?"

"Yes. I always go out for half an hour's walk after I've brought her down from her rest, and Mrs. Mackenzie usually spent the afternoon in her room. She used to take mother round the garden just before tea if I was out, otherwise I did that."

"Like clockwork?"

"Yes."

"I see. So there was half an hour in which Mrs. Ludlow could go to the hall, fetch the pills, hide them in her stick, and be found calmly playing patience as expected by whoever came home first?"

"I suppose so. It could have been like that," Phyllis said.

"When Mrs. Ludlow moved so instinctively to collect her stick it answered another question," Patrick said. "I never saw her without it; she must have been greatly attached to it."

"It was my father's," Gerald said. "She used it as a reinforcement to her bell."

"The gelatine capsules must have been emptied before the powder was administered," said Patrick. "To an able-bodied person, disposing of them would have been no problem, but Mrs. Ludlow would have found this difficult, dependent as she was on help throughout the day. If she swallowed them, she probably managed only one or two at a time. I reasoned that some might still be left. As it turned out, she had kept some whole capsules too, for herself, I imagine, if things went wrong. And she also took out another form of insurance. Do you know what was in the letter to the vicar, Mrs. Medhurst?"

"No. But he spoke to me after the service on Sunday. He seemed overcome with gratitude about something and said he'd be coming to see Mother. She made me ring up and tell him not to. She wouldn't even let him come to talk about Mrs. Mackenzie, or arrange about the funeral."

"I think you'll find she sent him a substantial cheque," said Patrick. "Doubtless your church needs funds."

There was a silence.

"She was neat with her hands, in spite of being so crippled," Patrick said. "I noticed that she could use a knife and fork, and so on, without any difficulty. Undoing the capsules and collecting up the powder, in an envelope, perhaps, would not have been a problem."

"If only I hadn't come," Helen cried. "None of this need have happened."

"Life can't be lived like that, Mrs. Ludlow," said Patrick gently.

"It's happened," Phyllis said. "Nothing can be undone. You mustn't look back, Helen. You and Gerald can have a happy life. After all, that's what poor Mother was trying to make sure of."

"What will happen now?" Cathy asked.

As she said this, the telephone rang.

"That may be your answer," Patrick said. He stood up as Jane went out of the room to see who it was. They heard her voice, murmuring, in the hall, and then she came back. She looked at Phyllis.

"I'm sorry," she said. "Mrs. Ludlow's dead. She never woke at all."

VI

After the Ludlows had all gone away, Jane and Patrick sat on by the dying embers of the fire. They were silent for a long time.

"I feel as if I'd swum the channel," Jane said at last. "Limp, and wrung out."

"Poor old thing. You had to bear the brunt, today," said Patrick.

"That wasn't so bad. I like Helen, and golly, am I sorry for her! What a life she's had. She adores Gerald, too. Funny, isn't it? He seems rather dull to me. Andrew liked her. Maybe she'll have another infant herself, when this blows over."

"Maybe she will," said Patrick. "I wonder how they'll all make out. We shan't lose touch, if Tim stays up and Cathy comes up later."

"Will Tim stay? What if his father goes to gaol?"

"I don't suppose it will come to that in the end. And it will do Tim good to get illicit jobs in term, like driving grocery vans, and spend his vacation working on building sites. Cathy may change her mind, though. Something else may crop up for her before the summer."

"I think she'll persevere," said Jane. "She'd be a plus influence, too, among the dollies."

Patrick wondered to himself if Oxford would make Cathy, or if it would break her heart.

"What about the bank manager?" Jane added. "Will he come up to scratch? What's he like?"

"Solid and reliable, as you might expect. Just what Phyllis needs. He's got a grown-up family and several grandchildren."

"You've been to see him, I suppose? That's how you know all this?"

"Naturally. What do you expect?" said Patrick. In fac

Maurice had boldly telephoned Pantons, demanding to speak
to Phyllis, just as she was busy with the nurse getting her
unconscious mother into bed. Patrick had thought it wiser
not to say too much over the telephone; he had instead
visited Maurice Richards and told him just a few of the facts,
so that he might appreciate how serious things were, and
understand that Phyllis's own distress might inhibit her from
getting in touch. What she chose to tell him in the end was
up to her.

"Dr. Cupid Grant, eh?" said Jane. "A man of parts."

"Do you still think I interfered too much?" he asked.

Jane pondered, wrinkling up her nose.

"I don't know," she said at last. "As it happens, things
seem to have worked out for the best in a case of terrible
alternatives. But the police would have got there in the end,
wouldn't they? Or the old girl would have confessed after
Helen was arrested?"

"Who's to know?" said Patrick.

"What will happen now? Will the story all come out?"

"I doubt it," said Patrick. "The police are satisfied. I expect
the verdict on Mrs. Mackenzie will be death by misadventure."

"There won't be an inquest on Mrs. Ludlow?"

"No. At her age, anything could happen, and the doctor
saw her regularly."

"It's so sad," said Jane. "Poor old woman, she kept them all
on the hop, all her life, and yet she died alone, with only a
strange nurse and a policewoman there."

"I hope they sell that house," said Patrick, getting up. He
knocked his pipe out into the ashes of the fire. "It's packed
with grim associations for them now."

"What about Alec Mackenzie?"

"He's going back to Canada. It seems he's wanted to for
years, but his mother was against it. I suppose she thought
her past would find her out if she did. He thinks his kids will
have more opportunity over there, and there's his sister,
too."

"Canada's large enough. I'd have thought Mrs. Mackenzie
could have started again in another part of it," said Jane.

"She would have, if she'd known what lay in store for her,
no doubt," said Patrick dryly. "Come on, Jane, time for bed.
That nephew of mine will have you up at dawn, if I know
him. I don't want Michael hounding me for letting you get
exhausted in his absence."

"He'll be back next week," Jane said. She stood up and stretched, and her eyes darkened as she thought about her husband. Patrick regarded her affectionately. Michael was very nearly worthy of her, in his view, and that was praise indeed.

"Well, it hasn't been too dull for you, having me to stay, has it?" he said. He plumped up the cushion in his chair, put the guard in front of the fire, and waited for her to leave the room ahead of him.

"Oh no, brother dear," said Jane. "It has not been dull."

ABOUT THE AUTHOR

MARGARET YORKE was born in Surrey, England and now lives in a Buckinghamshire village. She published her first novel in 1957 and has since written numerous crime and suspense works, which have been published in almost a dozen countries. She was the 1979–1980 Chairman of the Crime Writers' Association.

"THE BEST POPULAR NOVEL TO BE PUBLISHED IN AMERICA SINCE *THE GODFATHER*."
—Stephen King

RED DRAGON
by Thomas Harris, author of BLACK SUNDAY

If you never thought a book could make you quake with fear, prepare yourself for RED DRAGON. For in its pages, you will meet a human monster, a tortured being driven by a force he cannot contain, who pleasures in viciously murdering happy families. When you discover how he chooses his victims, you will never feel safe again.

Buy this book at your local bookstore or use this handy coupon for ordering:

Bantam Books, Inc., Dept. RD, 414 East Golf Road, Des Plaines, Ill. 60016

Please send me _____ copies of RED DRAGON (#22746-7 · $3.95). I am enclosing $ _____ (please add $1.25 to cover postage and handling, send check or money order—no cash or C.O.D.'s please).

Mr/Mrs/Miss _____

Address _____

City _____ State/Zip _____

Please allow four to six weeks for delivery.
This offer expires 3/83.   RD—9/82

Inside Boston Doctor's Hospital, patients are dying.
No one knows why,
No one but . . .

THE SISTERHOOD

Nurses bound together in mercy. Pledged to end human suffering. Sworn to absolute secrecy. But, within the Sisterhood, evil blooms. Under the white glare of the operating room, patients survive the surgeon's knife. Then, in the dark hollow silence of the nighttime hospital, they die. Suddenly, inexplicably, horribly. No one knows why. No one but the Sisterhood.

One man, a tough, bright doctor, risks his career, his very life, to unmask the terrifying mystery. One woman, a beautiful and dedicated young nurse, unknowingly holds the answer. Together they will discover that no one is safe from . . .

THE SISTERHOOD

A Novel by
MICHAEL PALMER

"Compassion turns to terror . . . Riveting reading, I couldn't put it down."

—V. C. Andrews, author of *Flowers in the Attic*

Read THE SISTERHOOD (#22704–1 • $3.75), on sale September 1, 1982 wherever Bantam paperbacks are sold or order directly from Bantam by including $1.00 for postage and handling and sending a check to Bantam Books, Dept. SI, 414 East Golf Road, Des Plaines, Ill. 60016. Allow 4–6 weeks for delivery. This offer expires 3/83.

THE ULTIMATE MARRIAGE
OF LOVE AND TERROR

THE TRUE
BRIDE

By Thomas Altman
author of KISS DADDY GOODBYE

Something strange is happening to Ellen. Someone is watching her wherever she goes. At the supermarket. At the library. At the shopping mall. Ellen is eight months pregnant. And someone is trying to drive her crazy.

Buy THE TRUE BRIDE at your local bookstore or use this handy coupon for ordering:

Bantam Books, Inc., Dept. TB, 414 East Golf Road,
Des Plaines, Ill. 60016

Please send me _____ copies of THE TRUE BRIDE (22687-8 • $2.95).
I am enclosing $_____ (please add $1.25 to cover postage and handling, send check or money order—no cash or C.O.D.'s please).

Mr/Mrs/Miss_____

Address_____

City_____State/Zip_____

TB—10/82

Please allow four to six weeks for delivery. This offer expires 4/83.